GEMS

OF

MYSTERY

Lost Jewels from a More Elegant Age

Edited by Greg Fowlkes

GEMS OF MYSTERY

Lost Jewels from a More Elegant Age

© 2012 Resurrected Press
www.ResurrectedPress.com

Published by Resurrected Press

This classic book was handcrafted by Resurrected Press. Resurrected Press is dedicated to bringing high quality classic books back to the readers who enjoy them. These are not scanned versions of the originals, but, rather, quality checked and edited books meant to be enjoyed!

Please visit ResurrectedPress.com to view our entire catalogue!

ISBN 13: 978-1-937022-44-0

Printed in the United States of America

FOREWORD

Gems have always held a fascination for readers of mysteries, a attraction far beyond that of mere money, and the jewel thief is viewed as being at the pinnacle of the criminal hierarchy, the gentry of the underworld. And as for detectives, well, preventing the theft of a famous jewel or the recovery of such a gem adds to a sleuth's reputation far more than uncovering a foul murderer. It is only natural then, that the theft of jewels, be they diamonds, rubies, emeralds or pearls, should figure heavily in the fictional literature of crime, and this was true particularly in the era before the First World War.

This era was also a period when the short story played its most prominent role in the genre. With numerous weekly and monthly magazines vying for the best authors to write mystery and detective stories for their readership to peruse as they made their commutes via the railway from the suburbs to the city and back, some of the best examples of the form appeared during this period, presenting in a scant six to ten thousand words a puzzle, the detection, and solution of a succinct mystery.

Novels were to have their day as well in the period after the war when Agatha Christie, Freeman Wills Crofts, and Dorothy L. Sayers were to ply their craft during the "Golden Age" of British mysteries.

But there has always been a few good stories of intermediate length; not enough for a dedicated book, but too long to be considered "short" stories. This collection brings together three "gems" of that era, written by three of the best authors of the period.

Each story features a rare jewel; a diamond necklace fit for a Czarina, an exquisite ruby ring, a famous string of pearls. But these stories are about more than mere crime, for they also deal with romance, real or imaginary. Nor are they mere dry accounts, being told with all the wit and panache a good author can impart.

Resurrected Press is pleased to present for our readers these three entertaining if lately somewhat neglected tales of mystery, romance, and of course the gems.

Greg Fowlkes
Editor-In-Chief
Resurrected Press
www.ResurrectedPress.com

RESURRECTED PRESS CLASSIC
MYSTERY CATALOGUE

E. C. Bentley
Trent's Last Case: The Woman in Black

Ernest Bramah
Max Carrados Resurrected:
The Detective Stories of Max Carrados

Agatha Christie
The Secret Adversary
The Mysterious Affair at Styles

Octavus Roy Cohen
Midnight

Freeman Wills Croft
The Ponson Case
The Pit Prop Syndicate

J. S. Fletcher
The Herapath Property
The Rayner-Slade Amalgamation
The Chestermarke Instinct
The Paradise Mystery
Dead Men's Money
The Middle of Things
Ravensdene Court
Scarhaven Keep
The Orange-Yellow Diamond
The Middle Temple Murder
The Tallyrand Maxim
The Borough Treasurer
In the Mayor's Parlour
The Saftey Pin

Carolyn Wells
Vicky Van
The Man Who Fell Through the Earth
In the Onyx Lobby
Raspberry Jam
The Clue
The Room with the Tassels
The Vanishing of Betty Varian
The Mystery Girl
The White Alley
The Curved Blades
Anybody but Anne
The Bride of a Moment
Faulkner's Folly
The Diamond Pin
The Gold Bag
The Mystery of the Sycamore
The Come Backy

Raoul Whitfield
Death in a Bowl

Mildred A. Wirt
The Clock Strikes Thirteen
Clue of the Silken Ladder
The Cry at Midnight
Ghost Beyond the Gate
Guilt of the Brass Thieves
Hoofbeats on the Turnpike
The Secret Pact
Saboteurs on the River
Signal in the Dark
Voice from the Cave
Whispering Walls
The Wishing Well

And much more!
Visit ResurrectedPress.com for our complete catalogue

TABLE OF CONTENTS

In The Fog

By Richard Harding Davis

Originally Published 1901

IN THE FOG
BY RICHARD HARDING DAVIS

The fogs of London are notorious. This series of three interrelated stories told over port and cigars at one of the London's oldest and most exclusive private clubs begins with a young American naval officer lost in such a fog. In his attempt to ask directions he finds himself enveloped in a mystery as thick as the fog.

Richard Harding Davis was certainly no stranger to adventure, having served as a war correspondent in the three conflicts that punctuated the start of the twentieth century. Indeed, in many ways he was the very model of the dashing soldier of fortune, and was to use that term in the title of his novel *Soldiers of Fortune*.

With it's mysterious Russian Princess, diamonds intended as a gift to the Czarina of Russia, and a dead son of a peer, *In the Fog* certainly has its share of intrigue and adventure, but it is told with a light touch making it an entertaining read.

About the Author

Richard Harding Davis (April 18, 1864-April 11, 1916) was an American journalist and author. Born in Philadelphia, he came by his writing talents from his parents, as his mother was an author and his father a journalist and newspaper editor. He first attracted national attention with his articles on the Johnstown flood and went on to be a war correspondent during the Spanish-American, Boer and Russo-Japanese wars. He was a close friend of Theodore Roosevelt and helped to create the legend of the Rough Riders. He traveled widely in Central and South America and Africa and wrote extensively about his experiences. Much of his fiction is set in the various locales he visited as a journalist. He was married twice and died of a heart attack at the age of 51.

IN THE FOG

CHAPTER I

The Grill is the club most difficult of access in the world. To be placed on its rolls distinguishes the new member as greatly as though he had received a vacant Garter or had been caricatured in "Vanity Fair."

Men who belong to the Grill Club never mention that fact. If you were to ask one of them which clubs he frequents, he will name all save that particular one. He is afraid if he told you he belonged to the Grill, that it would sound like boasting.

The Grill Club dates back to the days when Shakespeare's Theatre stood on the present site of the "Times" office. It has a golden Grill which Charles the Second presented to the Club, and the original manuscript of "Tom and Jerry in London," which was bequeathed to it by Pierce Egan himself. The members, when they write letters at the Club, still use sand to blot the ink.

The Grill enjoys the distinction of having blackballed, without political prejudice, a Prime Minister of each party. At the same sitting at which one of these fell, it elected, on account of his brogue and his bulls, Quiller, Q. C., who was then a penniless barrister.

When Paul Preval, the French artist who came to London by
royal command to paint a portrait of the Prince of Wales, was
made an honorary member—only foreigners may be honorary
members—he said, as he signed his first wine card, "I would
rather see my name on that, than on a picture in the Louvre."

At which. Quiller remarked, "That is a devil of a compliment,
because the only men who can read their names in the Louvre
to-day have been dead fifty years."

On the night after the great fog of 1897 there were five
members in the Club, four of them busy with supper and one
reading in front of the fireplace. There is only one room to the
Club, and one long table. At the far end of the room the fire of
the grill glows red, and, when the fat falls, blazes into flame, and
at the other there is a broad bow window of diamond panes,
which looks down upon the street. The four men at the table
were strangers to each other, but as they picked at the grilled
bones, and sipped their Scotch and soda, they conversed with
such charming animation that a visitor to the Club, which does
not tolerate visitors, would have counted them as friends of long
acquaintance, certainly not as Englishmen who had met for the
first time, and without the form of an introduction. But it is the
etiquette and tradition of the Grill, that whoever enters it must
speak with whomever he finds there. It is to enforce this rule
that there is but one long table, and whether there are twenty
men at it or two, the waiters, supporting the rule, will place
them side by side.

For this reason the four strangers at supper were seated
together, with the candles grouped about them, and the long
length of the table cutting a white path through the outer gloom.

"I repeat," said the gentleman with the black pearl stud,
"that the days for romantic adventure and deeds of foolish
daring have passed, and that the fault lies with ourselves.
Voyages to the pole I do not catalogue as adventures. That
African explorer, young Chetney, who turned up yesterday after
he was supposed to have died in Uganda, did nothing
adventurous. He made maps and explored the sources of rivers.
He was in constant danger, but the presence of danger does not
constitute adventure. Were that so, the chemist who studies
high explosives, or who investigates deadly poisons, passes
through adventures daily. No, 'adventures are for the

adventurous.' But one no longer ventures. The spirit of it has died of inertia. We are grown too practical, too just, above all, too sensible. In this room, for instance, members of this Club have, at the sword's point, disputed the proper scanning of one of Pope's couplets. Over so weighty a matter as spilled Burgundy on a gentleman's cuff, ten men fought across this table, each with his rapier in one hand and a candle in the other. All ten were wounded. The question of the spilled Burgundy concerned but two of them. The eight others engaged because they were men of 'spirit.' They were, indeed, the first gentlemen of the day. To-night, were you to spill Burgundy on my cuff, were you even to insult me grossly, these gentlemen would not consider it incumbent upon them to kill each other. They would separate us, and to-morrow morning appear as witnesses against us at Bow Street. We have here to-night, in the persons of Sir Andrew and myself, an illustration of how the ways have changed."

The men around the table turned and glanced toward the gentleman in front of the fireplace. He was an elderly and somewhat portly person, with a kindly, wrinkled countenance, which wore continually a smile of almost childish confidence and good-nature. It was a face which the illustrated prints had made intimately familiar. He held a book from him at arm's-length, as if to adjust his eyesight, and his brows were knit with interest.

"Now, were this the eighteenth century," continued the gentleman with the black pearl, "when Sir Andrew left the Club to-night I would have him bound and gagged and thrown into a sedan chair. The watch would not interfere, the passers-by would take to their heels, my hired bullies and ruffians would convey him to some lonely spot where we would guard him until morning. Nothing would come of it, except added reputation to myself as a gentleman of adventurous spirit, and possibly an essay in the 'Tatler,' with stars for names, entitled, let us say, 'The Budget and the Baronet.'"

"But to what end, sir?" inquired the youngest of the members. "And why Sir Andrew, of all persons—why should you select him for this adventure?"

The gentleman with the black pearl shrugged his shoulders.

"It would prevent him speaking in the House to-night. The Navy Increase Bill," he added gloomily. "It is a Government measure, and Sir Andrew speaks for it. And so great is his influence and so large his following that if he does"—the gentleman laughed ruefully—"if he does, it will go through. Now, had I the spirit of our ancestors," he exclaimed, "I would bring

chloroform from the nearest chemist's and drug him in that chair. I would tumble his unconscious form into a hansom cab, and hold him prisoner until daylight. If I did, I would save the British taxpayer the cost of five more battleships, many millions of pounds."

The gentlemen again turned, and surveyed the baronet with freshened interest. The honorary member of the Grill, whose accent already had betrayed him as an American, laughed softly.

"To look at him now,"

he said, "one would not guess he was deeply concerned with the affairs of state."

The others nodded silently.

"He has not lifted his eyes from that book since we first entered," added the youngest member. "He surely cannot mean to speak to-night."

"Oh, yes, he will speak," muttered the one with the black pearl moodily. "During these last hours of the session the House sits late, but when the Navy bill comes up on its third reading he will be in his place—and he will pass it."

The fourth member, a stout and florid gentleman of a somewhat sporting appearance, in a short smoking-jacket and black tie, sighed enviously.

"Fancy one of us being as cool as that, if he knew he had to stand up within an hour and rattle off a speech in Parliament. I 'd be in a devil of a funk myself. And yet he is as keen over that book he's reading as though he had nothing before him until bedtime."

"Yes, see how eager he is," whispered the youngest member. "He does not lift his eyes even now when he cuts the pages. It is probably an Admiralty Report, or some other weighty work of statistics which bears upon his speech."

The gentleman with the black pearl laughed morosely.

"The weighty work in which the eminent statesman is so deeply engrossed," he said, "is called 'The Great Rand Robbery.' It is a detective novel, for sale at all bookstalls."

The American raised his eyebrows in disbelief.

"'The Great Rand Robbery'?" he repeated incredulously. "What an odd taste!"

"It is not a taste, it is his vice," returned the gentleman with the pearl stud. "It is his one dissipation. He is noted for it. You, as a stranger, could hardly be expected to know of this idiosyncrasy. Mr. Gladstone sought relaxation in the Greek poets, Sir Andrew finds his in Gaboriau. Since I have been a member of Parliament I have never seen him in the library without a shilling shocker in his hands. He brings them even into the sacred precincts of the House, and from the Government benches reads them concealed inside his hat. Once started on a tale of murder, robbery, and sudden death, nothing can tear him from it, not even the call of the division bell, nor of hunger, nor the prayers of the party Whip. He gave up his country house because when he journeyed to it in the train he would become so absorbed in his detective stories that he was invariably carried past his station." The member of Parliament twisted his pearl stud nervously, and bit at the edge of his mustache. "If it only were the first pages of 'The Rand Robbery' that he were reading," he murmured bitterly, "instead of the last! With such another book as that, I swear I could hold him here until morning. There would be no need of chloroform to keep him from the House."

The eyes of all were fastened upon Sir Andrew, and each saw with fascination that with his forefinger he was now separating the last two pages of the book. The member of Parliament struck the table softly with his open palm.

"I would give a hundred pounds," he whispered, "if I could place in his hands at this moment a new story of Sherlock Holmes—a thousand pounds," he added wildly—"five thousand pounds!"

The American observed the speaker sharply, as though the words bore to him some special application, and then at an idea which apparently had but just come to him, smiled in great embarrassment.

Sir Andrew ceased reading, but, as though still under the influence of the book, sat looking blankly into the open fire. For a brief space no one moved until the baronet withdrew his eyes and, with a sudden start of recollection, felt anxiously for his watch. He scanned its face eagerly, and scrambled to his feet.

The voice of the American instantly broke the silence in a high, nervous accent.

"And yet Sherlock Holmes himself," he cried, "could not decipher the mystery which to-night baffles the police of London."

At these unexpected words, which carried in them something of the tone of a challenge, the gentlemen about the table started as suddenly as though the American had fired a pistol in the air, and Sir Andrew halted abruptly and stood observing him with grave surprise.

The gentleman with the black pearl was the first to recover.

"Yes, yes," he said eagerly, throwing himself across the table. "A mystery that baffles the police of London.

"I have heard nothing of it. Tell us at once, pray do—tell us at once."

The American flushed uncomfortably, and picked uneasily at the tablecloth.

"No one but the police has heard of it," he murmured, "and they only through me. It is a remarkable crime, to, which, unfortunately, I am the only person who can bear witness. Because I am the only witness, I am, in spite of my immunity as a diplomat, detained in London by the authorities of Scotland Yard. My name," he said, inclining his head politely, "is Sears, Lieutenant Ripley Sears of the United States Navy, at present Naval Attache to the Court of Russia. Had I not been detained to-day by the police I would have started this morning for Petersburg."

The gentleman with the black pearl interrupted with so  pronounced an exclamation of excitement and delight that the American stammered and ceased speaking.

"Do you hear, Sir Andrew!" cried the member of Parliament jubilantly. "An American diplomat halted by our police because he is the only witness of a most remarkable crime—*the* most remarkable crime, I believe you said, sir," he added, bending eagerly toward the naval officer, "which has occurred in London in many years."

The American moved his head in assent and glanced at the two other members. They were looking doubtfully at him, and the face of each showed that he was greatly perplexed.

Sir Andrew advanced to within the light of the candles and drew a chair toward him.

"The crime must be exceptional indeed," he said, "to justify the police in interfering with a representative of a friendly power. If I were not forced to leave at once, I should take the liberty of asking you to tell us the details."

The gentleman with the pearl pushed the chair toward Sir Andrew, and motioned him to be seated.

"You cannot leave us now," he exclaimed. "Mr. Sears is just about to tell us of this remarkable crime."

He nodded vigorously at the naval officer and the American, after first glancing doubtfully toward the servants at the far end of the room, leaned forward across the table. The others drew their chairs nearer and bent toward him. The baronet glanced irresolutely at his watch, and with an exclamation of annoyance snapped down the lid. "They can wait," he muttered. He seated himself quickly and nodded at Lieutenant Sears.

"If you will be so kind as to begin, sir," he said impatiently.

"Of course," said the American, "you understand that I understand that I am speaking to gentlemen. The confidences of this Club are inviolate. Until the police give the facts to the public press, I must consider you my confederates. You have heard nothing, you know no one connected with this mystery. Even I must remain anonymous."

The gentlemen seated around him nodded gravely.

"Of course," the baronet assented with eagerness, "of course."

"We will refer to it," said the gentleman with the black pearl, "as 'The Story of the Naval Attache.'"

"I arrived in London two days ago," said the American, "and I engaged a room at the Bath Hotel. I know very few people in London, and even the members of our embassy were strangers to me. But in Hong Kong I had become great pals with an officer in your navy, who has since retired, and who is now living in a small house in Rutland Gardens opposite the Knights-bridge barracks. I telegraphed him that I was in London, and yesterday morning I received a most hearty invitation to dine with him the same evening at his house. He is a bachelor, so we dined alone and talked over all our old days on the Asiatic Station, and of the changes which had come to us since we had last met there. As I was leaving the next morning for my post at Petersburg, and had many letters to write, I told him, about ten o'clock, that I must get back to the hotel, and he sent out his servant to call a hansom.

"For the next quarter of an hour, as we sat talking, we could hear the cab whistle sounding violently from the doorstep, but apparently with no result.

"'It cannot be that the cabmen are on strike,' my friend said, as he rose and walked to the window.

"He pulled back the curtains and at once called to me.

"'You have never seen a London fog, have you?' he asked. 'Well, come here. This is one of the best, or, rather, one of the worst, of them.' I joined him at the window, but I could see nothing. Had I not known that the house looked out upon the street I would have believed that I was facing a dead wall. I raised the sash and stretched out my head, but still I could see nothing. Even the light of the street lamps opposite, and in the upper windows of the barracks, had been smothered in the yellow mist. The lights of the room in which I stood penetrated the fog only to the distance of a few inches from my eyes.

"Below me the servant was still sounding his whistle, but I could afford to wait no longer, and told my friend that I would try and find the way to my hotel on foot. He objected, but the letters I had to write were for the Navy Department, and, besides, I had always heard that to be out in a London fog was the most wonderful experience, and I was curious to investigate one for myself.

"My friend went with me to his front door, and laid down a course for me to follow. I was first to walk straight across the street to the brick wall of the Knightsbridge Barracks. I was then to feel my way along the wall until I came to a row of houses set back from the sidewalk. They would bring me to a cross street. On the other side of this street was a row of shops which I was to follow until they joined the iron railings of Hyde Park. I was to keep to the railings until I reached the gates at Hyde Park Corner, where I was to lay a diagonal course across Piccadilly, and tack in toward the railings of Green Park. At the end of these railings, going east, I would find the Walsingham, and my own hotel.

"To a sailor the course did not seem difficult, so I bade my friend goodnight and walked forward until my feet touched the paving. I continued upon it until I reached the curbing of the sidewalk. A few steps further, and my hands struck the wall of the barracks. I turned in the direction from which I had just come, and saw a square of faint light cut in the yellow fog. I shouted 'All right,' and the voice of my friend answered, 'Good luck to you.' The light from his open door disappeared with a bang, and I was left alone in a dripping, yellow darkness. I have been in the Navy for ten years, but I have never known such a fog as that of last night, not even among the icebergs of Behring Sea. There one at least could see the light of the binnacle, but last night I could not even distinguish the hand by which I guided myself along the barrack wall. At sea a fog is a natural phenomenon. It is as familiar as the rainbow which follows a storm, it is as proper that a fog should spread upon the waters as that steam shall rise from a kettle. But a fog which springs from the paved streets, that rolls between solid house-fronts, that forces cabs to move at half speed, that drowns policemen and extinguishes the electric lights of the music hall, that to me is incomprehensible. It is as out of place as a tidal wave on Broadway.

"As I felt my way along the wall, I encountered other men who were coming from the opposite direction, and each time when we hailed each other I stepped away from the wall to make room for them to pass. But the third time I did this, when I reached out my hand, the wall had disappeared, and the further I moved to find it the further I seemed to be sinking into space. I had the unpleasant conviction that at any moment I might step over a precipice. Since I had set out I had heard no traffic in the street, and now, although I listened some minutes, I could only distinguish the occasional footfalls of pedestrians. Several times I called aloud, and once a jocular gentleman answered me, but only to ask me where I thought he was, and then even he was swallowed up in the silence. Just above me I could make out a jet of gas which I guessed came from a street lamp, and I moved over to that, and, while I tried to recover my bearings, kept my hand on the iron post. Except for this flicker of gas, no larger than the tip of my finger, I could distinguish nothing about me. For the rest, the mist hung between me and the world like a damp and heavy blanket.

"I could hear voices, but I could not tell from whence they came, and the scrape of a foot moving cautiously, or a muffled cry as some one stumbled, were the only sounds that reached me.

"I decided that until some one took me in tow I had best remain where I was, and it must have been for ten minutes that I waited by the lamp, straining my ears and hailing distant footfalls. In a house near me some people were dancing to the music of a Hungarian band. I even fancied I could hear the windows shake to the rhythm of their feet, but I could not make out from which part of the compass the sounds came. And sometimes, as the music rose, it seemed close at my hand, and again, to be floating high in the air above my head. Although I was surrounded by thousands of householders—13—I was as completely lost as though I had been set down by night in the Sahara Desert. There seemed to be no reason in waiting longer for an escort, so I again set out, and at once bumped against a low iron fence. At first I believed this to be an area railing, but on following it I found that it stretched for a long distance, and that it was pierced at regular intervals with gates. I was standing uncertainly with my hand on one of these when a square of light suddenly opened in the night, and in it I saw, as you see a picture thrown by a biograph in a darkened theatre, a young gentleman in evening dress, and back of him the lights of a hall. I guessed from its elevation and distance from the sidewalk that this light must come from the door of a house set back from the street, and I determined to approach it and ask the young man to tell me where I was. But in fumbling with the lock of the gate I instinctively bent my head, and when I raised it again the door had partly closed, leaving only a narrow shaft of light. Whether the young man had re-entered the house, or had left it I could not tell, but I hastened to open the gate, and as I stepped forward I found myself upon an asphalt walk. At the same instant there was the sound of quick steps upon the path, and some one rushed past me. I called to him, but he made no reply, and I heard the gate click and the footsteps hurrying away upon the sidewalk.

"Under other circumstances the young man's rudeness, and his recklessness in dashing so hurriedly through the mist, would have struck me as peculiar, but everything was so distorted by the fog that at the moment I did not consider it. The door was still as he had left it, partly open. I went up the path, and, after much fumbling, found the knob of the door-bell and gave it a sharp pull. The bell answered me from a great depth and distance, but no movement followed from inside the house, and although I pulled the bell again and again I could hear nothing save the dripping of the mist about me. I was anxious to be on my way, but unless I knew where I was going there was little chance of my making any speed, and I was determined that until I learned my bearings I would not venture back into the fog. So I pushed the door open and stepped into the house.

"I found myself in a long and narrow hall, upon which doors opened from either side. At the end of the hall was a staircase with a balustrade which ended in a sweeping curve. The balustrade was covered with heavy Persian rugs, and the walls of the hall were also hung with them. The door on my left was closed, but the one nearer me on the right was open, and as I stepped opposite to it I saw that it was a sort of reception or waiting-room, and that it was empty. The door below it was also open, and with the idea that I would surely find some one there,

I walked on up the hall. I was in evening dress, and I felt I did not look like a burglar, so I had no great fear that, should I encounter one of the inmates of the house, he would shoot me on sight. The second door in the hall opened into a dining-room. This was also empty. One person had been dining at the table, but the cloth had not been cleared away, and a nickering candle showed half-filled wineglasses and the ashes of cigarettes. The greater part of the room was in complete darkness.

"By this time I had grown conscious of the fact that I was wandering about in a strange house, and that, apparently, I was alone in it. The silence of the place began to try my nerves, and in a sudden, unexplainable panic I started for the open street. But as I turned, I saw a man sitting on a bench, which the curve of the balustrade had hidden from me. His eyes were shut, and he was sleeping soundly.

"The moment before I had been bewildered because I could see no one, but at sight of this man I was much more bewildered.

"He was a very large man, a giant in height, with long yellow hair which hung below his shoulders. He was dressed in a red silk shirt that was belted at the waist and hung outside black velvet trousers which, in turn, were stuffed into high black boots. I recognized the costume at once as that of a Russian servant, but what a Russian servant in his native livery could be doing in a private house in Knightsbridge was incomprehensible.

"I advanced and touched the man on the shoulder, and after an effort he awoke, and, on seeing me, sprang to his feet and began bowing rapidly and making deprecatory gestures. I had picked up enough Russian in Petersburg to make out that the man was apologizing for having fallen asleep, and I also was able to explain to him that I desired to see his master.

"He nodded vigorously, and said, 'Will the Excellency come this way? The Princess is here.'

"I distinctly made out the word 'princess,' and I was a good deal embarrassed. I had thought it would be easy enough to explain my intrusion to a man, but how a woman would look at it was another matter, and as I followed him down the hall I was somewhat puzzled.

"As we advanced, he noticed that the front door was standing open, and with an exclamation of surprise, hastened toward it and closed it. Then he rapped twice on the door of what was apparently the drawing-room. There was no reply to his knock, and he tapped again, and then timidly, and cringing subserviently, opened the door and stepped inside. He withdrew himself at once and stared stupidly at me, shaking his head.

"'She is not there,' he said. He stood for a moment gazing blankly through the open door, and then hastened toward the dining-room. The solitary candle which still burned there seemed to assure him that the room also was empty. He came back and bowed me toward the drawing-room. 'She is above,' he said; 'I will inform the Princess of the Excellency's presence.'

"Before I could stop him he had turned and was running up the staircase, leaving me alone at the open door of the drawing-room. I decided that the adventure had gone quite far enough, and if I had been able to explain to the Russian that I had lost my way in the fog, and only wanted to get back into the street again, I would have left the house on the instant.

"Of course, when I first rang the bell of the house I had no other expectation than that it would be answered by a parlor-maid who would direct me on my way. I certainly could not then foresee that I would disturb a Russian princess in her boudoir, or that I might be thrown out by her athletic bodyguard. Still, I thought I ought not now to leave the house without making some apology, and, if the worst should come, I could show my card. They could hardly believe that a member of an Embassy had any designs upon the hat-rack.

"The room in which I stood was dimly lighted, but I could see that, like the hall, it was hung with heavy Persian rugs. The corners were filled with palms, and there was the unmistakable odor in the air of Russian cigarettes, and strange, dry scents that carried me back to the bazaars of Vladivostock. Near the front windows was a grand piano, and at the other end of the room a heavily carved screen of some black wood, picked out with ivory. The screen was overhung with a canopy of silken draperies, and formed a sort of alcove. In front of the alcove was spread the white skin of a polar bear, and set on that was one of those low Turkish coffee tables. It held a lighted spirit-lamp and two gold coffee cups. I had heard no movement from above stairs, and it must have been fully three minutes that I stood waiting, noting these details of the room and wondering at the delay, and at the strange silence.

"And then, suddenly, as my eye grew more used to the half-light, I saw, projecting from behind the screen as though it were stretched along the back of a divan, the hand of a man and the lower part of his arm. I was as startled as though I had come across a footprint on a deserted island. Evidently the man had been sitting there since I had come into the room, even since I had entered the house, and he had heard the servant knocking upon the door. Why he had not declared himself I could not understand, but I supposed that possibly he was a guest, with no reason to interest himself in the Princess's other visitors, or perhaps, for some reason, he did not wish to be observed. I could see nothing of him except his hand, but I had an unpleasant feeling that he had been peering at me through the carving in the screen, and that he still was doing so. I moved my feet noisily on the floor and said tentatively, 'I beg your pardon.'

"There was no reply, and the hand did not stir. Apparently the man was bent upon ignoring me, but as all I wished was to apologize for my intrusion and to leave the house, I walked up to the alcove and peered around it. Inside the screen was a divan piled with cushions, and on the end of it nearer me the man was sitting. He was a young Englishman with light yellow hair and a deeply bronzed face.

"He was seated with his arms stretched out along the back of the divan, and with his head resting against a cushion. His attitude was one of complete ease. But his mouth had fallen open, and his eyes were set with an expression of utter horror. At the first glance I saw that he was quite dead.

"For a flash of time I was too startled to act, but in the same flash I was convinced that the man had met his death from no accident, that he had not died through any ordinary failure of the laws of nature. The expression on his face was much too terrible to be misinterpreted. It spoke as eloquently as words. It told me that before the end had come he had watched his death approach and threaten him.

"I was so sure he had been murdered that I instinctively looked on the floor for the weapon, and, at the same moment, out of concern for my own safety, quickly behind me; but the silence of the house continued unbroken.

"I have seen a great number of dead men; I was on the Asiatic Station during the Japanese-Chinese war. I was in Port

Arthur after the massacre. So a dead man, for the single reason that he is dead, does not repel me, and, though I knew that there was no hope that this man was alive, still for decency's sake, I felt his pulse, and while I kept my ears alert for any sound from the floors above me, I pulled open his shirt and placed my hand upon his heart. My fingers instantly touched upon the opening of a wound, and as I withdrew them I found them wet with blood. He was in evening dress, and in the wide bosom of his shirt I found a narrow slit, so narrow that in the dim light it was scarcely discernable. The wound was no wider than the smallest blade of a pocket-knife, but when I stripped the shirt away from the chest and left it bare, I found that the weapon, narrow as it was, had been long enough to reach his heart. There is no need to tell you how I felt as I stood by the body of this boy, for he was hardly older than a boy, or of the thoughts that came into my head. I was bitterly sorry for this stranger, bitterly indignant at his murderer, and, at the same time, selfishly concerned for my own safety and for the notoriety which I saw was sure to follow. My instinct was to leave the body where it lay, and to hide myself in the fog, but I also felt that since a succession of accidents had made me the only witness to a crime, my duty was to make myself a good witness and to assist to establish the facts of this murder.

"That it might possibly be a suicide, and not a murder, did not disturb me for a moment. The fact that the weapon had disappeared, and the expression on the boy's face were enough to convince, at least me, that he had had no hand in his own death. I judged it, therefore, of the first importance to discover who was in the house, or, if they had escaped from it, who had been in the house before I entered it. I had seen one man leave it; but all I could tell of him was that he was a young man, that he was in evening dress, and that he had fled in such haste that he had not stopped to close the door behind him.

"The Russian servant I had found apparently asleep, and, unless he acted a part with supreme skill, he was a stupid and ignorant boor, and as innocent of the murder as myself. There was still the Russian princess whom he had expected to find, or had pretended to expect to find, in the same room with the murdered man. I judged that she must now be either upstairs with the servant, or that she had, without his knowledge, already fled from the house. When I recalled his apparently genuine surprise at not finding her in the drawing-room, this latter supposition seemed the more probable. Nevertheless, I decided that it was my duty to make a search, and after a second hurried look for the weapon among the cushions of the divan, and upon the floor, I cautiously crossed the hall and entered the dining-room.

"The single candle was still flickering in the draught, and showed only the white cloth. The rest of the room was draped in shadows. I picked up the candle, and, lifting it high above my head, moved around the corner of the table. Either my nerves were on such a stretch that no shock could strain them further, or my mind was inoculated to horrors, for I did not cry out at what I saw nor retreat from it. Immediately at my feet was the body of

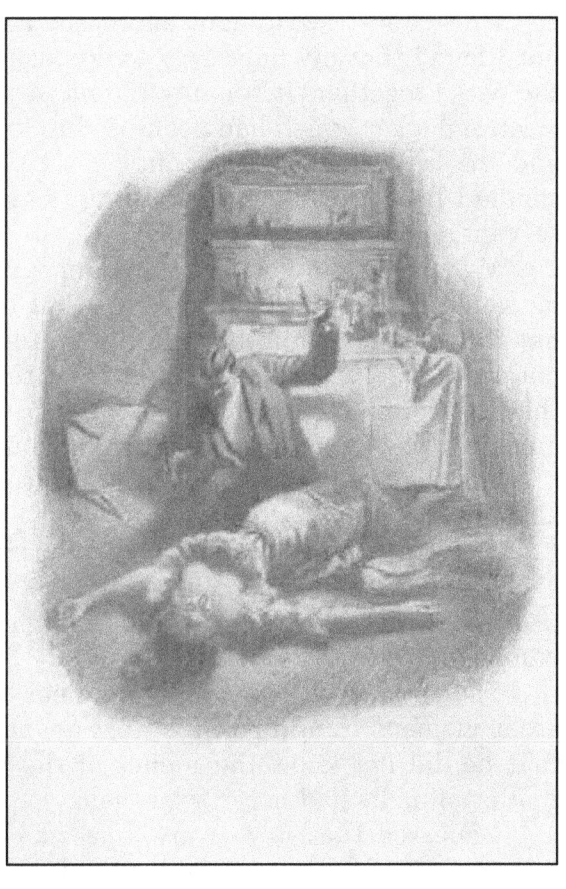

a beautiful woman, lying at full length upon the floor, her arms flung out on either side of her, and her white face and shoulders gleaming dully in the unsteady light of the candle. Around her throat was a great chain of diamonds, and the light played upon these and made them flash and blaze in tiny flames. But the woman who wore them was dead, and I was so certain as to how she had died that without an instant's hesitation I dropped on my knees beside her and placed my hands above her heart. My fingers again touched the thin slit of a wound. I had no doubt in my mind but that this was the Russian princess, and when I lowered the candle to her face I was assured that this was so. Her features showed the finest lines of both the Slav and the Jewess; the eyes were black, the hair blue-black and wonderfully heavy, and her skin, even in death, was rich in color. She was a surpassingly beautiful woman.

"I rose and tried to light another candle with the one I held, but I found that my hand was so unsteady that I could not keep the wicks together. It was my intention to again search for this strange dagger which had been used to kill both the English boy and the beautiful princess, but before I could light the second candle I heard footsteps descending the stairs, and the Russian servant appeared in the doorway.

"My face was in darkness, or I am sure that at the sight of it he would have taken alarm, for at that moment I was not sure but that this man himself was the murderer. His own face was plainly visible to me in the light from the hall, and I could see that it wore an expression of dull bewilderment. I stepped quickly toward him and took a firm hold upon his wrist.

"'She is not there,' he said. 'The Princess has gone. They have all gone.'

"'Who have gone?' I demanded. 'Who else has been here?'

"'The two Englishmen,' he said.

"'What two Englishmen?' I demanded. 'What are their names?'

"The man now saw by my manner that some question of great moment hung upon his answer, and he began to protest that he did not know the names of the visitors and that until that evening he had never seen them.

"I guessed that it was my tone which frightened him, so I took my hand off his wrist and spoke less eagerly.

"'How long have they been here?' I asked, 'and when did they go?'

"He pointed behind him toward the drawing-room.

"'One sat there with the Princess,' he said; 'the other came after I had placed the coffee in the drawing-room. The two Englishmen talked together and the Princess returned here to the table. She sat there in that chair, and I brought her cognac and cigarettes. Then I sat outside upon the bench. It was a feast day, and I had been drinking. Pardon, Excellency, but I fell asleep. When I woke, your Excellency was standing by me, but the Princess and the two Englishmen had gone. That is all I know.'

"I believed that the man was telling me the truth. His fright had passed, and he was now apparently puzzled, but not alarmed.

"'You must remember the names of the Englishmen,' I urged. 'Try to think. When you announced them to the Princess what name did you give?'

"At this question he exclaimed with pleasure, and, beckoning to me, ran hurriedly down the hall and into the drawing-room. In the corner furthest from the screen was the piano, and on it was a silver tray. He picked this up and, smiling with pride at his own intelligence, pointed at two cards that lay upon it. I took them up and read the names engraved upon them."

The American paused abruptly, and glanced at the faces about him. "I read the names," he repeated. He spoke with great reluctance.

"Continue!" cried the Baronet, sharply.

"I read the names," said the American with evident distaste, "and the family name of each was the same. They were the names of two brothers. One is well known to you. It is that of the African explorer of whom this gentleman was just speaking. I mean the Earl of Chetney. The other was the name of his brother, Lord Arthur Chetney."

The men at the table fell back as though a trapdoor had fallen open at their feet.

"Lord Chetney!" they exclaimed in chorus. They glanced at each other and back to the American with every expression of concern and disbelief.

"It is impossible!" cried the Baronet. "Why, my dear sir, young Chetney only arrived from Africa yesterday. It was so stated in the evening papers."

The jaw of the American set in a resolute square, and he pressed his lips together.

"You are perfectly right, sir," he said, "Lord Chetney did arrive in London yesterday morning, and yesterday night I found his dead body."

The youngest member present was the first to recover. He seemed much less concerned over the identity of the murdered man than at the interruption of the narrative.

"Oh, please let him go on!" he cried. "What happened then? You say you found two visiting cards. How do you know which card was that of the murdered man?"

The American, before he answered, waited until the chorus of exclamations had ceased. Then he continued as though he had not been interrupted.

"The instant I read the names upon the cards," he said, "I ran to the screen and, kneeling beside the dead man, began a search through his pockets. My hand at once fell upon a card-case, and I found on all the cards it contained the title of the Earl of Chetney. His watch and cigarette-case also bore his name. These evidences, and the fact of his bronzed skin, and that his cheekbones were worn with fever, convinced me that the dead man was the African explorer, and the boy who had fled past me in the night was Arthur, his younger brother.

"I was so intent upon my search that I had forgotten the servant, and I was still on my knees when I heard a cry behind me. I turned, and saw the man gazing down at the body in abject horror.

"Before I could rise, he gave another cry of terror, and, flinging himself into the hall, raced toward the door to the street. I leaped after him, shouting to him to halt, but before I could reach the hall he had torn open the door, and I saw him spring out into the yellow fog. I cleared the steps in a jump and ran down the garden walk but just as the gate clicked in front of me. I had it open on the instant, and, following the sound of the man's footsteps, I raced after him across the open street. He, also, could hear me, and he instantly stopped running, and there was absolute silence. He was so near that I almost fancied I could hear him panting, and I held my own breath to listen. But I could distinguish nothing but the dripping of the mist about us, and from far off the music of the Hungarian band, which I had heard when I first lost myself.

"All I could see was the square of light from the door I had left open behind me, and a lamp in the hall beyond it flickering in the draught. But even as I watched it, the flame of the lamp was blown violently to and fro, and the door, caught in the same current of air, closed slowly. I knew if it shut I could not again enter the house, and I rushed madly toward it. I believe I even shouted out, as though it were something human which I could compel to obey me, and then I caught my foot against the curb and smashed into the sidewalk. When I rose to my feet I was dizzy and half stunned, and though I thought then that I was moving toward the door, I know now that I probably turned directly from it; for, as I groped about in the night, calling frantically for the police, my fingers touched nothing but the dripping fog, and the iron railings for which I sought seemed to have melted away. For many minutes I beat the mist with my arms like one at blind man's buff, turning sharply in circles, cursing aloud at my stupidity and crying continually for help. At last a voice answered me from the fog, and I found myself held in the circle of a policeman's lantern.

"That is the end of my adventure. What I have to tell you now is what I learned from the police.

"At the station-house to which the man guided me I related what you have just heard. I told them that the house they must at once find was one set back from the street within a radius of two hundred yards from the Knightsbridge Barracks, that within fifty yards of it some one was giving a dance to the music of a Hungarian band, and that the railings before it were as high as a man's waist and filed to a point. With that to work upon, twenty men were at once ordered out into the fog to search for the house, and Inspector Lyle himself was despatched to the home of Lord Edam, Chetney's father, with a warrant for Lord Arthur's arrest. I was thanked and dismissed on my own recognizance.

"This morning, Inspector Lyle called on me, and from him I learned the police theory of the scene I have just described.

"Apparently I had wandered very far in the fog, for up to noon to-day the house had not been found, nor had they been able to arrest Lord Arthur. He did not return to his father's house last night, and there is no trace of him; but from what the police knew of the past lives of the people I found in that lost house, they have evolved a theory, and their theory is that the murders were committed by Lord Arthur.

"The infatuation of his elder brother, Lord Chetney, for a Russian princess, so Inspector Lyle tells me, is well known to every one. About two years ago the Princess Zichy, as she calls herself, and he were constantly together, and Chetney informed his friends that they were about to be married. The woman was notorious in two continents, and when Lord Edam heard of his son's infatuation he appealed to the police for her record.

"It is through his having applied to them that they know so much concerning her and her relations with the Chetneys. From the police Lord Edam learned that Madame Zichy had once been a spy in the employ of the Russian Third Section, but that lately she had been repudiated by her own government and was living by her wits, by blackmail, and by her beauty. Lord Edam laid this record before his son, but Chetney either knew it already or the woman persuaded him not to believe in it, and the father and son parted in great anger. Two days later the marquis altered his will, leaving all of his money to the younger brother, Arthur.

"The title and some of the landed property he could not keep from Chetney, but he swore if his son saw the woman again that the will should stand as it was, and he would be left without a penny.

"This was about eighteen months ago, when apparently Chetney tired of the Princess, and suddenly went off to shoot and explore in Central Africa. No word came from him, except that twice he was reported as having died of fever in the jungle, and finally two traders reached the coast who said they had seen his body. This was accepted by all as conclusive, and young Arthur was recognized as the heir to the Edam millions. On the strength of this supposition he at once began to borrow enormous sums from the money lenders. This is of great importance, as the police believe it was these debts which drove him to the murder of his brother. Yesterday, as you know, Lord Chetney suddenly returned from the grave, and it was the fact that for two years he had been considered as dead which lent such importance to his return and which gave rise to those columns of detail concerning him which appeared in all the afternoon papers. But, obviously, during his absence he had not tired of the Princess Zichy, for we know that a few hours after he reached London he sought her out. His brother, who had also learned of his reappearance through the papers, probably suspected which would be the house he would first visit, and followed him there, arriving, so the Russian servant tells us, while the two were at coffee in the drawing-room. The Princess, then, we also learn from the servant, withdrew to the dining-room, leaving the brothers together. What happened one can only guess.

"Lord Arthur knew now that when it was discovered he was no longer the heir, the money-lenders would come down upon him. The police believe that he at once sought out his brother to beg for money to cover the post-obits, but that, considering the sum he needed was several hundreds of thousands of pounds, Chetney refused to give it him. No one knew that Arthur had gone to seek out his brother. They were alone. It is possible, then, that in a passion of disappointment, and crazed with the disgrace which he saw before him, young Arthur made himself the heir beyond further question. The death of his brother would have availed nothing if the woman remained alive. It is then possible that he crossed the hall, and with the same weapon which made him Lord Edam's heir destroyed the solitary witness to the murder. The only other person who could have seen it was sleeping in a drunken stupor, to which fact undoubtedly he owed his life. And yet," concluded the Naval Attache, leaning forward and marking each word with his finger, "Lord Arthur blundered fatally. In his haste he left the door of the house open, so giving access to the first passer-by, and he forgot that when he entered it he had handed his card to the servant. That piece of paper may yet send him to the gallows. In the mean time he has disappeared completely, and somewhere, in one of the millions of streets of this great capital, in a locked and empty house, lies the body of his brother, and of the woman his brother loved, undiscovered, unburied, and with their murder unavenged."

In the discussion which followed the conclusion of the story of the Naval Attache the gentleman with the pearl took no part. Instead, he arose, and, beckoning a servant to a far corner of the room, whispered earnestly to him until a sudden movement on the part of Sir Andrew caused him to return hurriedly to the table.

"There are several points in Mr. Sears's story I want explained," he cried. "Be seated, Sir Andrew," he begged. "Let us have the opinion of an expert. I do not care what the police think, I want to know what you think."

But Sir Henry rose reluctantly from his chair.

"I should like nothing better than to discuss this," he said. "But it is most important that I proceed to the House. I should have been there some time ago." He turned toward the servant and directed him to call a hansom.

The gentleman with the pearl stud looked appealingly at the Naval Attache. "There are surely many details that you have not told us," he urged. "Some you have forgotten."

The Baronet interrupted quickly.

"I trust not," he said, "for I could not possibly stop to hear them."

"The story is finished," declared the Naval Attache; "until Lord Arthur is arrested or the bodies are found there is nothing more to tell of either Chetney or the Princess Zichy."

"Of Lord Chetney perhaps not," interrupted the sporting-looking gentleman with the black tie, "but there'll always be something to tell of the Princess Zichy. I know enough stories about her to fill a book. She was a most remarkable woman." The speaker dropped the end of his cigar into his coffee cup and, taking his case from his pocket, selected a fresh one. As he did so he laughed and held up the case that the others might see it. It was an ordinary cigar-case of well-worn pig-skin, with a silver clasp.

"The only time I ever met her," he said, "she tried to rob me of this."

The Baronet regarded him closely.

"She tried to rob you?" he repeated.

"Tried to rob me of this," continued the gentleman in the black tie, "and of the Czarina's diamonds." His tone was one of mingled admiration and injury.

"The Czarina's diamonds!" exclaimed the Baronet. He glanced quickly and suspiciously at the speaker, and then at the others about the table. But their faces gave evidence of no other emotion than that of ordinary interest.

"Yes, the Czarina's diamonds," repeated the man with the black tie. "It was a necklace of diamonds. I was told to take them to the Russian Ambassador in Paris who was to deliver them at Moscow. I am a Queen's Messenger," he added.

"Oh, I see," exclaimed Sir Andrew in a tone of relief. "And you say that this same Princess Zichy, one of the victims of this double murder, endeavored to rob you of—of—that cigar-case."

"And the Czarina's diamonds," answered the Queen's Messenger imperturbably. "It's not much of a story, but it gives you an idea of the woman's character. The robbery took place between Paris and Marseilles."

The Baronet interrupted him with an abrupt movement. "No, no," he cried, shaking his head in protest. "Do not tempt me. I really cannot listen. I must be at the House in ten minutes."

"I am sorry," said the Queen's Messenger. He turned to those seated about him. "I wonder if the other gentlemen—" he inquired tentatively. There was a chorus of polite murmurs, and the Queen's Messenger, bowing his head in acknowledgment, took a preparatory sip from his glass. At the same moment the servant to whom the man with the black pearl had spoken, slipped a piece of paper into his hand. He glanced at it, frowned, and threw it under the table.

The servant bowed to the Baronet.

"Your hansom is waiting, Sir Andrew," he said.

"The necklace was worth twenty thousand pounds," began the Queen's Messenger. "It was a present from the Queen of England to celebrate—" The Baronet gave an exclamation of angry annoyance.

"Upon my word, this is most provoking," he interrupted. "I really ought not to stay. But I certainly mean to hear this." He turned irritably to the servant. "Tell the hansom to wait," he commanded, and, with an air of a boy who is playing truant, slipped guiltily into his chair.

The gentleman with the black pearl smiled blandly, and rapped upon the table.

"Order, gentlemen," he said. "Order for the story of the Queen's Messenger and the Czarina's diamonds."

CHAPTER II

"The necklace was a present from the Queen of England to the Czarina of Russia," began the Queen's Messenger. "It was to celebrate the occasion of the Czar's coronation. Our Foreign Office knew that the Russian Ambassador in Paris was to proceed to Moscow for that ceremony, and I was directed to go to Paris and turn over the necklace to him. But when I reached Paris I found he had not expected me for a week later and was taking a few days' vacation at Nice. His people asked me to leave the necklace with them at the Embassy, but I had been charged to get a receipt for it from the Ambassador himself, so I started at once for Nice The fact that Monte Carlo is not two thousand miles from Nice may have had something to do with making me carry out my instructions so carefully. Now, how the Princess Zichy came to find out about the necklace I don't know, but I can guess. As you have just heard, she was at one time a spy in the service of the Russian government. And after they dismissed her she kept up her acquaintance with many of the Russian agents in London. It is probable that through one of them she learned that the necklace was to be sent to Moscow, and which one of the Queen's Messengers had been detailed to take it there. Still, I doubt if even that knowledge would have helped her if she had not also known something which I supposed no one else in the world knew but myself and one other man. And, curiously enough, the other man was a Queen's Messenger too, and a friend of mine. You must know that up to the time of this robbery I had always concealed my despatches in a manner peculiarly my own. I got the idea from that play called 'A Scrap of Paper.' In it a man wants to hide a certain compromising document. He knows that all his rooms will be secretly searched for it, so he puts it in a torn envelope and sticks it up where any one can see it on his mantel shelf. The result is that the woman who is ransacking the house to find it looks in all the unlikely places, but passes over the scrap of paper that is just under her nose. Sometimes the papers and packages they give us to carry about Europe are of very great value, and sometimes they are special makes of cigarettes, and orders to court dressmakers. Sometimes we know what we are carrying and sometimes we do not. If it is a large sum of money or a treaty, they generally tell us. But, as a rule, we have no knowledge of what the package contains; so, to be on the safe side, we naturally take just as great care of it as though we knew it held the terms of an ultimatum or the crown jewels. As a rule, my confreres carry the official packages in a despatch-box, which is just as obvious as a lady's jewel bag in the hands of her maid. Every one knows they are carrying something of value. They put a premium on dishonesty. Well, after I saw the 'Scrap of Paper' play, I determined to put the government valuables in the most unlikely place that any one would look for them. So I used to hide the documents they gave me inside my riding-boots, and small articles, such as money or jewels, I carried in an old cigar-case. After I took to using my case for that purpose I bought a new one, exactly like it, for my cigars. But to avoid mistakes, I had my initials placed on both sides of the new one, and the moment I touched the case, even in the dark, I could tell which it was by the raised initials.

"No one knew of this except the Queen's Messenger of whom I spoke. We once left Paris together on the Orient Express. I was going to Constantinople and he was to stop off at Vienna. On the journey I told him of my peculiar way of hiding things and showed him my cigar-case. If I recollect rightly, on that trip it held the grand cross of St. Michael and St. George, which the Queen was sending to our Ambassador. The Messenger was very much entertained at my scheme, and some months later when he met the Princess he told her about it as an amusing story. Of course, he had no idea she was a Russian spy. He didn't know anything at all about her, except that she was a very attractive woman.

"It was indiscreet, but he could not possibly have guessed that she could ever make any use of what he told her.

"Later, after the robbery, I remembered that I had informed this young chap of my secret hiding-place, and when I saw him again I questioned him about it. He was greatly distressed, and said he had never seen the importance of the secret. He remembered he had told several people of it, and among others the Princess Zichy. In that way I found out that it was she who had robbed me, and I know that from the moment I left London she was following me and that she knew then that the diamonds were concealed in my cigar-case.

"My train for Nice left Paris at ten in the morning. When I travel at night I generally tell the *chef de gare* that I am a Queen's Messenger, and he gives me a compartment to myself, but in the daytime I take whatever offers. On this morning I had found an empty compartment, and I had tipped the guard to keep every one else out, not from any fear of losing the diamonds, but because I wanted to smoke. He had locked the door, and as the last bell had rung I supposed I was to travel alone, so I began to arrange my traps and make myself comfortable. The diamonds in the cigar-case were in the inside pocket of my waistcoat, and as they made a bulky package, I took them out, intending to put them in my hand bag. It is a small satchel like a bookmaker's, or those hand bags that couriers carry. I wear it slung from a strap across my shoulder, and, no matter whether I am sitting or walking, it never leaves me.

"I took the cigar-case which held the necklace from my inside pocket and the case which held the cigars out of the satchel, and while I was searching through it for a box of matches I laid the two cases beside me on the seat.

"At that moment the train started, but at the same instant there was a rattle at the lock of the compartment, and a couple of porters lifted and shoved a woman through the door, and hurled her rugs and umbrellas in after her.

"Instinctively I reached for the diamonds. I shoved them quickly into the satchel and, pushing them far down to the bottom of the bag, snapped the spring lock. Then I put the cigars in the pocket of my coat, but with the thought that now that I had a woman as a travelling companion I would probably not be allowed to enjoy them.

"One of her pieces of luggage had fallen at my feet, and a roll of rugs had landed at my side. I thought if I hid the fact that the lady was not welcome, and at once endeavored to be civil, she might permit me to smoke. So I picked her hand bag off the floor and asked her where I might place it.

"As I spoke I looked at her for the first time, and saw that she was a most remarkably handsome woman.

"She smiled charmingly and begged me not to disturb myself. Then she arranged her own things about her, and, opening her dressing-bag, took out a gold cigarette case.

"'Do you object to smoke?' she asked.

"I laughed and assured her I had been in great terror lest she might object to it herself.

"'If you like cigarettes,' she said, 'will you try some of these? They are rolled especially for my husband in Russia, and they are supposed to be very good.'

"I thanked her, and took one from her case, and I found it so much better than my own that I continued to smoke her cigarettes throughout the rest of the journey. I must say that we got on very well. I judged from the coronet on her cigarette-case, and from her manner, which was quite as well bred as that of any woman I ever met, that she was some one of importance, and though she seemed almost too good looking to be respectable, I determined that she was some *grande dame* who was so assured of her position that she could afford to be unconventional. At first she read her novel, and then she made some comment on the scenery, and finally we began to discuss the current politics of the Continent. She talked of all the cities in Europe, and seemed to know every one worth knowing. But she volunteered nothing about herself except that she frequently made use of the expression, 'When my husband was stationed at Vienna,' or 'When my husband was promoted to Rome.' Once she said to me, 'I have often seen you at Monte Carlo. I saw you when you won the pigeon championship.' I told her that I was not a pigeon shot, and she gave a little start of surprise. 'Oh, I beg your pardon,' she said; 'I thought you were Morton Hamilton, the English champion.' As a matter of fact, I do look like Hamilton, but I know now that her object was to make me think that she had no idea as to who I really was. She needn't have acted at all, for I certainly had no suspicions of her, and was only too pleased to have so charming a companion.

"The one thing that should have made me suspicious was the fact that at every station she made some trivial excuse to get me out of the compartment. She pretended that her maid was travelling back of us in one of the second-class carriages, and kept saying she could not imagine why the woman did not come to look after her, and if the maid did not turn up at the next stop, would I be so very kind as to get out and bring her whatever it was she pretended she wanted.

"I had taken my dressing-case from the rack to get out a novel, and had left it on the seat opposite to mine, and at the end of the compartment farthest from her. And once when I came back from buying her a cup of chocolate, or from some other fool errand, I found her standing at my end of the compartment with both hands on the dressing-bag. She looked at me without so much as winking an eye, and shoved the case carefully into a corner. 'Your bag slipped off on the floor,' she said. 'If you've got any bottles in it, you had better look and see that they're not broken.'

"And I give you my word, I was such an ass that I did open the case and looked all through it. She must have thought I *was* a Juggins. I get hot all over whenever I remember it. But in spite of my dulness, and her cleverness, she couldn't gain anything by sending me away, because what she wanted was in the hand bag and every time she sent me away the hand bag went with me.

"After the incident of the dressing-case her manner changed. Either in my absence she had had time to look through it, or, when I was examining it for broken bottles, she had seen everything it held.

"From that moment she must have been certain that the cigar-case, in which she knew I carried the diamonds, was in the bag that was fastened to my body, and from that time on she probably was plotting how to get it from me. Her anxiety became most apparent. She dropped the great lady manner, and her charming condescension went with it. She ceased talking, and, when I spoke, answered me irritably, or at random. No doubt her mind was entirely occupied with her plan. The end of our journey was drawing rapidly nearer, and her time for action was being cut down with the speed of the express train. Even I, unsuspicious as I was, noticed that something was very wrong with her. I really believe that before we reached Marseilles if I had not, through my own stupidity, given her the chance she wanted, she might have stuck a knife in me and rolled me out on the rails. But as it was, I only thought that the long journey had tired her. I suggested that it was a very trying trip, and asked her if she would allow me to offer her some of my cognac.

"She thanked me and said, 'No,' and then suddenly her eyes lighted, and she exclaimed, 'Yes, thank you, if you will be so kind.'

"My flask was in the hand bag, and I placed it on my lap and with my thumb slipped back the catch. As I keep my tickets and railroad guide in the bag, I am so constantly opening it that I never bother to lock it, and the fact that it is strapped to me has always been sufficient protection. But I can appreciate now what a satisfaction, and what a torment too, it must have been to that woman when she saw that the bag opened without a key.

"While we were crossing the mountains I had felt rather chilly and had been wearing a light racing coat. But after the lamps were lighted the compartment became very hot and stuffy, and I found the coat uncomfortable. So I stood up, and, after first slipping the strap of the bag over my head, I placed the bag in the seat next me and pulled off the racing coat. I don't blame myself for being careless; the bag was still within reach of my hand, and nothing would have happened if at that exact moment the train had not stopped at Arles. It was the combination of my removing the bag and our entering the station at the same instant which gave the Princess Zichy the chance she wanted to rob me.

"I needn't say that she was clever enough to take it. The train ran into the station at full speed and came to a sudden stop. I had just thrown my coat into the rack, and had reached out my hand for the bag. In another instant I would have had the strap around my shoulder. But at that moment the Princess threw open the door of the compartment and beckoned wildly at the people on the platform. 'Natalie!' she called, 'Natalie! here I am. Come here! This way!' She turned upon me in the greatest excitement. 'My maid!' she cried. 'She is looking for me. She passed the window without seeing me. Go, please, and bring her back.' She continued pointing out of the door and beckoning me with her other hand. There certainly was something about that woman's tone which made one jump. When she was giving orders you had no chance to think of anything else. So I rushed out on my errand of mercy, and then rushed back again to ask what the maid looked like.

"'In black,' she answered, rising and blocking the door of the compartment. 'All in black, with a bonnet!'

"The train waited three minutes at Aries, and in that time I suppose I must have rushed up to over twenty women and asked, 'Are you Natalie?' The only reason I wasn't punched with an umbrella or handed over to the police was that they probably thought I was crazy.

"When I jumped back into the compartment the Princess was seated where I had left her, but her eyes were burning with happiness. She placed her hand on my arm almost affectionately, and said in a hysterical way, 'You are very kind to me. I am so sorry to have troubled you.'

"I protested that every woman on the platform was dressed in black.

"'Indeed I am so sorry,' she said, laughing; and she continued to laugh until she began to breathe so quickly that I thought she was going to faint.

"I can see now that the last part of that journey must have been a terrible half hour for her. She had the cigar-case safe enough, but she knew that she herself was not safe. She understood if I were to open my bag, even at the last minute, and miss the case, I would know positively that she had taken it. I had placed the diamonds in the bag at the very moment she entered the compartment, and no one but our two selves had occupied it since. She knew that when we reached Marseilles she would either be twenty thousand pounds richer than when she left Paris, or that she would go to jail. That was the situation as

she must have read it, and I don't envy her her state of mind during that last half hour. It must have been hell.

"I saw that something was wrong, and in my innocence I even wondered if possibly my cognac had not been a little too strong. For she suddenly developed into a most brilliant conversationalist, and applauded and laughed at everything I said, and fired off questions at me like a machine gun, so that I had no time to think of anything but of what she was saying. Whenever I stirred she stopped her chattering and leaned toward me, and watched me like a cat over a mouse-hole. I wondered how I could have considered her an agreeable travelling companion. I thought I would have preferred to be locked in with a lunatic. I don't like to think how she would have acted if I had made a move to examine the bag, but as I had it safely strapped around me again, I did not open it, and I reached Marseilles alive. As we drew into the station she shook hands with me and grinned at me like a Cheshire cat.

"'I cannot tell you,' she said, 'how much I have to thank you for.' What do you think of that for impudence!

"I offered to put her in a carriage, but she said she must find Natalie, and that she hoped we would meet again at the hotel. So I drove off by myself, wondering who she was, and whether Natalie was not her keeper.

"I had to wait several hours for the train to Nice, and as I wanted to stroll around the city I thought I had better put the diamonds in the safe of the hotel. As soon as I reached my room I locked the door, placed the hand bag on the table and opened it. I felt among the things at the top of it, but failed to touch the cigar-case. I shoved my hand in deeper, and stirred the things about, but still I did not reach it. A cold wave swept down my spine, and a sort of emptiness came to the pit of my stomach. Then I turned red-hot, and the sweat sprung out all over me. I wet my lips with my tongue, and said to myself, 'Don't be an ass. Pull yourself together, pull yourself together. Take the things out, one at a time. It's there, of course it's there. Don't be an ass.'

"So I put a brake on my nerves and began very carefully to pick out the things one by one, but after another second I could not stand it, and I rushed across the room and threw out everything on the bed. But the diamonds were not among them. I pulled the things about and tore them open and shuffled and rearranged and sorted them, but it was no use. The cigar-case was gone. I threw everything in the dressing-case out on the floor, although I knew it was useless to look for it there. I knew that I had put it in the bag. I sat down and tried to think. I remembered I had put it in the satchel at Paris just as that woman had entered the compartment, and I had been alone with her ever since, so it was she who had robbed me. But how? It had never left my shoulder. And then I remembered that it had— that I had taken it off when I had changed my coat and for the few moments that I was searching for Natalie. I remembered that the woman had sent me on that goose chase, and that at every other station she had tried to get rid of me on some fool errand.

"I gave a roar like a mad bull, and I jumped down the stairs six steps at a time.

"I demanded at the office if a distinguished lady of title, possibly a Russian, had just entered the hotel.

"As I expected, she had not. I sprang into a cab and inquired at two other hotels, and then I saw the folly of trying to catch her without outside help, and I ordered the fellow to gallop to the office of the Chief of Police. I told my story, and the ass in charge asked me to calm myself, and wanted to take notes. I told him this was no time for taking notes, but for doing something. He got wrathy at that, and I demanded to be taken at once to his

Chief. The Chief, he said, was very busy, and could not see me. So I showed him my silver greyhound. In eleven years I had never used it but once before. I stated in pretty vigorous language that I was a Queen's Messenger, and that if the Chief of Police did not see me instantly he would lose his official head. At that the fellow jumped off his high horse and ran with me to his Chief,—a smart young chap, a colonel in the army, and a very intelligent man.

"I explained that I had been robbed in a French railway carriage of a diamond necklace belonging to the Queen of England, which her Majesty was sending as a present to the Czarina of Russia. I pointed out to him that if he succeeded in capturing the thief he would be made for life, and would receive the gratitude of three great powers.

"He wasn't the sort that thinks second thoughts are best. He saw Russian and French decorations sprouting all over his chest, and he hit a bell, and pressed buttons, and yelled out orders like the captain of a penny steamer in a fog. He sent her description to all the city gates, and ordered all cabmen and railway porters to search all trains leaving Marseilles. He ordered all passengers on outgoing vessels to be examined, and telegraphed the proprietors of every hotel and pension to send him a complete list of their guests within the hour. While I was standing there he must have given at least a hundred orders, and sent out enough commissaires, sergeants de ville, gendarmes, bicycle police, and plain-clothes Johnnies to have captured the entire German army. When they had gone he assured me that the woman was as good as arrested already. Indeed, officially, she was arrested; for she had no more chance of escape from Marseilles than from the Chateau D'If.

"He told me to return to my hotel and possess my soul in peace. Within an hour he assured me he would acquaint me with her arrest.

"I thanked him, and complimented him on his energy, and left him. But I didn't share in his confidence. I felt that she was a very clever woman, and a match for any and all of us. It was all very well for him to be jubilant. He had not lost the diamonds, and had everything to gain if he found them; while I, even if he did recover the necklace, would only be where I was before I lost them, and if he did not recover it I was a ruined man. It was an awful facer for me. I had always prided myself on my record. In eleven years I had never mislaid an envelope, nor missed taking the first train. And now I had failed in the most important mission that had ever been intrusted to me. And it wasn't a thing that could be hushed up, either. It was too conspicuous, too spectacular. It was sure to invite the widest notoriety. I saw myself ridiculed all over the Continent, and perhaps dismissed, even suspected of having taken the thing myself.

"I was walking in front of a lighted cafe, and I felt so sick and miserable that I stopped for a pick-me-up. Then I considered that if I took one drink I would probably, in my present state of mind, not want to stop under twenty, and I decided I had better leave it alone. But my nerves were jumping like a frightened rabbit, and I felt I must have something to quiet them, or I would go crazy. I reached for my cigarette-case, but a cigarette seemed hardly adequate, so I put it back again and took out this cigar-case, in which I keep only the strongest and blackest cigars. I opened it and stuck in my fingers, but instead of a cigar they touched on a thin leather envelope. My heart stood perfectly still. I did not dare to look, but I dug my finger nails into the leather and I felt layers of thin paper, then a layer of cotton, and then they scratched on the facets of the Czarina's diamonds!

"I stumbled as though I had been hit in the face, and fell back into one of the chairs on the sidewalk. I tore off the wrappings and spread out the diamonds on the cafe table; I could not believe they were real. I twisted the necklace between my fingers and crushed it between my palms and tossed it up in the air. I believe I almost kissed it. The women in the cafe stood tip on the chairs to see better, and laughed and screamed, and the people crowded so close around me that the waiters had to form a bodyguard. The proprietor thought there was a fight, and called for the police. I was so happy I didn't care. I laughed, too, and gave the proprietor a five-pound note, and told him to stand every one a drink. Then I tumbled into a fiacre and galloped off to my friend the Chief of Police. I felt very sorry for him. He had been so happy at the chance I gave him, and he was sure to be disappointed when he learned I had sent him off on a false alarm.

"But now that I had found the necklace, I did not want him to find the woman. Indeed, I was most anxious that she should get clear away, for if she were caught the truth would come out, and I was likely to get a sharp reprimand, and sure to be laughed at.

"I could see now how it had happened. In my haste to hide the diamonds when the woman was hustled into the carriage, I had shoved the cigars into the satchel, and the diamonds into the pocket of my coat. Now that I had the diamonds safe again, it seemed a very natural mistake. But I doubted if the Foreign Office would think so. I was afraid it might not appreciate the beautiful simplicity of my secret hiding-place. So, when I reached the police station, and found that the woman was still at large, I was more than relieved.

"As I expected, the Chief was extremely chagrined when he learned of my mistake, and that there was nothing for him to do. But I was feeling so happy myself that I hated to have any one else miserable, so I suggested that this attempt to steal the Czarina's necklace might be only the first of a series of such attempts by an unscrupulous gang, and that I might still be in danger.

"I winked at the Chief and the Chief smiled at me, and we went to Nice together in a saloon car with a guard of twelve carabineers and twelve plain-clothes men, and the Chief and I drank champagne all the way. We marched together up to the hotel where the Russian Ambassador was stopping, closely surrounded by our escort of carabineers, and delivered the necklace with the most profound ceremony. The old Ambassador was immensely impressed, and when we hinted that already I had been made the object of an attack by robbers, he assured us that his Imperial Majesty would not prove ungrateful.

"I wrote a swinging personal letter about the invaluable services of the Chief to the French Minister of Foreign Affairs, and they gave him enough Russian and French medals to satisfy even a French soldier. So, though he never caught the woman, he received his just reward."

The Queen's Messenger paused and surveyed the faces of those about him in some embarrassment.

"But the worst of it is," he added, "that the story must have got about; for, while the Princess obtained nothing from me but a cigar-case and five excellent cigars, a few weeks after the coronation the Czar sent me a gold cigar-case with his monogram in diamonds. And I don't know yet whether that was a coincidence, or whether the Czar wanted me to know that he knew that I had been carrying the Czarina's diamonds in my pigskin cigar-case. What do you fellows think?"

CHAPTER III

Sir Andrew rose with disapproval written in every lineament.

"I thought your story would bear upon the murder," he said. "Had I imagined it would have nothing whatsoever to do with it I would not have remained." He pushed back his chair and bowed stiffly. "I wish you good night," he said.

There was a chorus of remonstrance, and under cover of this and the Baronet's answering protests a servant for the second time slipped a piece of paper into the hand of the gentleman with the pearl stud. He read the lines written upon it and tore it into tiny fragments.

The youngest member, who had remained an interested but silent listener to the tale of the Queen's Messenger, raised his hand commandingly.

"Sir Andrew," he cried, "in justice to Lord Arthur Chetney I must ask you to be seated. He has been accused in our hearing of a most serious crime, and I insist that you remain until you have heard me clear his character."

"You!" cried the Baronet.

"Yes," answered the young man briskly. "I would have spoken sooner," he explained, "but that I thought this gentleman"—he inclined his head toward the Queen's Messenger—"was about to contribute some facts of which I was ignorant. He, however, has told us nothing, and so I will take up the tale at the point where Lieutenant Sears laid it down and give you those details of which Lieutenant Sears is ignorant. It seems strange to you that I should be able to add the sequel to this story. But the coincidence is easily explained. I am the junior member of the law firm of Chudleigh & Chudleigh. We have been solicitors for the Chetneys for the last two hundred years. Nothing, no matter how unimportant, which concerns Lord Edam and his two sons is unknown to us, and naturally we are acquainted with every detail of the terrible catastrophe of last night."

The Baronet, bewildered but eager, sank back into his chair.

"Will you be long, sir!" he demanded.

"I shall endeavor to be brief," said the young solicitor; "and," he added, in a tone which gave his words almost the weight of a threat, "I promise to be interesting."

"There is no need to promise that," said Sir Andrew, "I find it much too interesting as it is." He glanced ruefully at the clock and turned his eyes quickly from it.

"Tell the driver of that hansom," he called to the servant, "that I take him by the hour."

"For the last three days," began young Mr. Chudleigh, "as you have probably read in the daily papers, the Marquis of Edam has been at the point of death, and his physicians have never left his house. Every hour he seemed to grow weaker; but although his bodily strength is apparently leaving him forever, his mind has remained clear and active. Late yesterday evening word was received at our office that he wished my father to come at once to Chetney House and to bring with him certain papers. What these papers were is not essential; I mention them only to explain how it was that last night I happened to be at Lord Edam's bed-side. I accompanied my father to Chetney House, but at the time we reached there Lord Edam was sleeping, and his physicians refused to have him awakened. My father urged that he should be allowed to receive Lord Edam's instructions concerning the documents, but the physicians would not disturb him, and we all gathered in the library to wait until he should awake of his own accord. It was about one o'clock in the morning, while we were still there, that Inspector Lyle and the officers from Scotland Yard came to arrest Lord Arthur on the charge of murdering his brother. You can imagine our dismay and distress. Like every one else, I had learned from the afternoon papers that Lord Chetney was not dead, but that he had returned to England, and on arriving at Chetney House I had been told that Lord Arthur had gone to the Bath Hotel to look for his brother and to inform him that if he wished to see their father alive he must come to him at once. Although it was now past one o'clock, Arthur had not returned. None of us knew where Madame Zichy lived, so we could not go to recover Lord Chetney's body. We spent a most miserable night, hastening to the window whenever a cab came into the square, in the hope that it was Arthur returning, and endeavoring to explain away the facts that pointed to him as the murderer. I am a friend of

Arthur's, I was with him at Harrow and at Oxford, and I refused to believe for an instant that he was capable of such a crime; but as a lawyer I could not help but see that the circumstantial evidence was strongly against him.

"Toward early morning Lord Edam awoke, and in so much better a state of health that he refused to make the changes in the papers which he had intended, declaring that he was no nearer death than ourselves. Under other circumstances, this happy change in him would have relieved us greatly, but none of us could think of anything save the death of his elder son and of the charge which hung over Arthur.

"As long as Inspector Lyle remained in the house my father decided that I, as one of the legal advisers of the family, should also remain there. But there was little for either of us to do. Arthur did not return, and nothing occurred until late this morning, when Lyle received word that the Russian servant had been arrested. He at once drove to Scotland Yard to question him. He came back to us in an hour, and informed me that the servant had refused to tell anything of what had happened the night before, or of himself, or of the Princess Zichy. He would not even give them the address of her house.

"'He is in abject terror,' Lyle said. 'I assured him that he was not suspected of the crime, but he would tell me nothing.'

"There were no other developments until two o'clock this afternoon, when word was brought to us that Arthur had been found, and that he was lying in the accident ward of St. George's Hospital. Lyle and I drove there together, and found him propped up in bed with his head bound in a bandage. He had been brought to the hospital the night before by the driver of a hansom that had run over him in the fog. The cab-horse had kicked him on the head, and he had been carried in unconscious. There was nothing on him to tell who he was, and it was not until he came to his senses this afternoon that the hospital authorities had been able to send word to his people. Lyle at once informed him that he was under arrest, and with what he was charged, and though the inspector warned him to say nothing which might be used against him, I, as his solicitor, instructed him to speak freely and to tell us all he knew of the occurrences of last night. It was evident to any one that the fact of his brother's death was of much greater concern to him, than that he was accused of his murder.

"'That,' Arthur said contemptuously, 'that is damned nonsense. It is monstrous and cruel. We parted better friends than we have been in years. I will tell you all that happened— not to clear myself, but to help you to find out the truth.' His story is as follows: Yesterday afternoon, owing to his constant attendance on his father, he did not look at the evening papers, and it was not until after dinner, when the butler brought him one and told him of its contents, that he learned that his brother was alive and at the Bath Hotel. He drove there at once, but was told that about eight o'clock his brother had gone out, but without giving any clew to his destination. As Chetney had not at once come to see his father, Arthur decided that he was still angry with him, and his mind, turning naturally to the cause of their quarrel, determined him to look for Chetney at the home of the Princess Zichy.

"Her house had been pointed out to him, and though he had never visited it, he had passed it many times and knew its exact location. He accordingly drove in that direction, as far as the fog would permit the hansom to go, and walked the rest of the way, reaching the house about nine o'clock. He rang, and was admitted by the Russian servant. The man took his card into the drawing-room, and at once his brother ran out and welcomed him. He was followed by the Princess Zichy, who also received Arthur most cordially.

"'You brothers will have much to talk about,' she said. 'I am going to the dining-room. When you have finished, let me know.'

"As soon as she had left them, Arthur told his brother that their father was not expected to outlive the night, and that he must come to him at once.

"'This is not the moment to remember your quarrel,' Arthur said to him; 'you have come back from the dead only in time to make your peace with him before he dies.'

"Arthur says that at this Chetney was greatly moved.

"'You entirely misunderstand me, Arthur,' he returned. 'I did not know the governor was ill, or I would have gone to him the instant I arrived. My only reason for not doing so was because I thought he was still angry with me. I shall return with you immediately, as soon as I have said good-by to the Princess. It is a final good-by. After tonight, I shall never see her again.'

"'Do you mean that?' Arthur cried.

"'Yes,' Chetney answered. 'When I returned to London I had no intention of seeking her again, and I am here only through a mistake.' He then told Arthur that he had separated from the Princess even before he went to Central Africa, and that, moreover, while at Cairo on his way south, he had learned certain facts concerning her life there during the previous season, which made it impossible for him to ever wish to see her again. Their separation was final and complete.

"'She deceived me cruelly,' he said; 'I cannot tell you how cruelly. During the two years when I was trying to obtain my father's consent to our marriage she was in love with a Russian diplomat. During all that time he was secretly visiting her here in London, and her trip to Cairo was only an excuse to meet him there.'

"'Yet you are here with her tonight,' Arthur protested, 'only a few hours after your return.'

"'That is easily explained,' Chetney answered. 'As I finished dinner tonight at the hotel, I received a note from her from this address. In it she said she had but just learned of my arrival, and begged me to come to her at once. She wrote that she was in great and present trouble, dying of an incurable illness, and without friends or money. She begged me, for the sake of old times, to come to her assistance. During the last two years in the jungle all my former feeling for Ziehy has utterly passed away, but no one could have dismissed the appeal she made in that letter. So I came here, and found her, as you have seen her, quite as beautiful as she ever was, in very good health, and, from the look of the house, in no need of money.

"'I asked her what she meant by writing me that she was dying in a garret, and she laughed, and said she had done so because she was afraid, unless I thought she needed help, I would not try to see her. That was where we were when you arrived. And now,' Chetney added, 'I will say good-by to her, and you had better return home. No, you can trust me, I shall follow you at once. She has no influence over me now, but I believe, in spite of the way she has used me, that she is, after her queer fashion, still fond of me, and when she learns that this good-by is final there may be a scene, and it is not fair to her that you should be here. So, go home at once, and tell the governor that I am following you in ten minutes.' "'That,' said Arthur, 'is the way we parted. I never left him on more friendly terms. I was happy to see him alive again, I was happy to think he had returned in time to make up his quarrel with my father, and I was happy that at last he was shut of that woman. I was never better pleased with him in my life.' He turned to Inspector Lyle, who was sitting at the foot of the bed taking notes of all he told us.

"'Why in the name of common sense,' he cried, 'should I have chosen that moment of all others to send my brother back to the grave!' For a moment the Inspector did not answer him. I do not know if any of you gentlemen are acquainted with Inspector Lyle, but if you are not, I can assure you that he is a very remarkable man. Our firm often applies to him for aid, and he has never failed us; my father has the greatest possible respect for him. Where he has the advantage over the ordinary police official is in the fact that he possesses imagination. He imagines himself to be the criminal, imagines how he would act under the same circumstances, and he imagines to such purpose that he generally finds the man he wants. I have often told Lyle that if he had not been a detective he would have made a great success as a poet, or a playwright.

"When Arthur turned on him Lyle hesitated for a moment, and then told him exactly what was the case against him.

"'Ever since your brother was reported as having died in Africa,' he said, 'your Lordship has been collecting money on post obits. Lord Chetney's arrival last night turned them into waste paper. You were suddenly in debt for thousands of pounds—for much more than you could ever possibly pay. No one knew that you and your brother had met at Madame Zichy's. But you knew that your father was not expected to outlive the night, and that if your brother were dead also, you would be saved from complete ruin, and that you would become the Marquis of Edam.'

"'Oh, that is how you have worked it out, is it?' Arthur cried. 'And for me to become Lord Edam was it necessary that the woman should die, too!'

"'They will say,' Lyle answered, 'that she was a witness to the murder—that she would have told.'

"'Then why did I not kill the servant as well!' Arthur said.

"'He was asleep, and saw nothing.'

"'And you believe *that?*' Arthur demanded.

"'It is not a question of what I believe,' Lyle said gravely. 'It is a question for your peers.'

"'The man is insolent!' Arthur cried. 'The thing is monstrous! Horrible!'

"Before we could stop him he sprang out of his cot and began pulling on his clothes. When the nurses tried to hold him down, he fought with them.

"'Do you think you can keep me here,' he shouted, 'when they are plotting to hang me? I am going with you to that house!' he cried at Lyle. 'When you find those bodies I shall be beside you. It is my right. He is my brother. He has been murdered, and I can tell you who murdered him. That woman murdered him. She first ruined his life, and now she has killed him. For the last five years she has been plotting to make herself his wife, and last night, when he told her he had discovered the truth about the Russian, and that she would never see him again, she flew into a passion and stabbed him, and then, in terror of the gallows, killed herself. She murdered him, I tell you, and I promise you that we will find the knife she used near her—perhaps still in her hand. What will you say to that?'

"Lyle turned his head away and stared down at the floor. 'I might say,' he answered, 'that you placed it there.'

"Arthur gave a cry of anger and sprang at him, and then pitched forward into his arms. The blood was running from the cut under the bandage, and he had fainted. Lyle carried him back to the bed again, and we left him with the police and the doctors, and drove at once to the address he had given us. We found the house not three minutes' walk from St. George's Hospital. It stands in Trevor Terrace, that little row of houses set back from Knightsbridge, with one end in Hill Street.

"As we left the hospital Lyle had said to me, 'You must not blame me for treating him as I did. All is fair in this work, and if by angering that boy I could have made him commit himself I was right in trying to do so; though, I assure you, no one would be better pleased than myself if I could prove his theory to be correct. But we cannot tell. Everything depends upon what we see for ourselves within the next few minutes.'

"When we reached the house, Lyle broke open the fastenings of one of the windows on the ground floor, and, hidden by the trees in the garden, we scrambled in. We found ourselves in the reception-room, which was the first room on the right of the hall. The gas was still burning behind the colored glass and red silk shades, and when the daylight streamed in after us it gave the hall a hideously dissipated look, like the foyer of a theatre at a matinee, or the entrance to an all-day gambling hell. The house was oppressively silent, and because we knew why it was so silent we spoke in whispers. When Lyle turned the handle of the drawing-room door, I felt as though some one had put his hand upon my throat. But I followed close at his shoulder, and saw, in the subdued light of many-tinted lamps, the body of Chetney at the foot of the divan, just as Lieutenant Sears had described it. In the drawing-room we found the body of the Princess Zichy, her arms thrown out, and the blood from her heart frozen in a tiny line across her bare shoulder. But neither of us, although we searched the floor on our hands and knees, could find the weapon which had killed her.

"'For Arthur's sake,' I said, 'I would have given a thousand pounds if we had found the knife in her hand, as he said we would.'

"'That we have not found it there,' Lyle answered, 'is to my mind the strongest proof that he is telling the truth, that he left the house before the murder took place. He is not a fool, and had he stabbed his brother and this woman, he would have seen that by placing the knife near her he could help to make it appear as if she had killed Chetney and then committed suicide. Besides,

Lord Arthur insisted that the evidence in his behalf would be our finding the knife here. He would not have urged that if he knew we would *not* find it, if he knew he himself had carried it away. This is no suicide. A suicide does not rise and hide the weapon with which he kills himself, and then lie down again. No, this has been a double murder, and we must look outside of the house for the murderer.'

"While he was speaking Lyle and I had been searching every corner, studying the details of each room. I was so afraid that, without telling me, he would make some deductions prejudicial to Arthur, that I never left his side. I was determined to see everything that he saw, and, if possible, to prevent his interpreting it in the wrong way. He finally finished his examination, and we sat down together in the drawing-room, and he took out his notebook and read aloud all that Mr. Sears had told him of the murder and what we had just learned from Arthur. We compared the two accounts word for word, and weighed statement with statement, but I could not determine from anything Lyle said which of the two versions he had decided to believe.

"'We are trying to build a house of blocks,' he exclaimed, 'with half of the blocks missing. We have been considering two theories,' he went on: 'one that Lord Arthur is responsible for both murders, and the other that the dead woman in there is responsible for one of them, and has committed suicide; but, until the Russian servant is ready to talk, I shall refuse to believe in the guilt of either.'

"'What can you prove by him!' I asked. 'He was drunk and asleep. He saw nothing.'

"Lyle hesitated, and then, as though he had made up his mind to be quite frank with me, spoke freely.

"'I do not know that he was either drunk or asleep,' he answered. 'Lieutenant Sears describes him as a stupid boor. I am not satisfied that he is not a clever actor. What was his position in this house! What was his real duty here? Suppose it was not to guard this woman, but to watch her. Let us imagine that it was not the woman he served, but a master, and see where that leads us. For this house has a master, a mysterious, absentee landlord, who lives in St. Petersburg, the unknown Russian who came between Chetney and Zichy, and because of whom Chetney left her. He is the man who bought this house for Madame Zichy, who sent these rugs and curtains from St. Petersburg to furnish it for her after his own tastes, and, I believe, it was he also who placed the Russian servant here, ostensibly to serve the Princess, but in reality to spy upon her. At Scotland Yard we do not know who this gentleman is; the Russian police confess to equal ignorance concerning him. When Lord Chetney went to Africa, Madame Zichy lived in St. Petersburg; but there her receptions and dinners were so crowded with members of the nobility and of the army and diplomats, that among so many visitors the police could not learn which was the one for whom she most greatly cared.'

"Lyle pointed at the modern French paintings and the heavy silk rugs which hung upon the walls.

"'The unknown is a man of taste and of some fortune,' he said, 'not the sort of man to send a stupid peasant to guard the woman he loves. So I am not content to believe, with Mr. Sears, that the servant is a boor. I believe him instead to be a very clever ruffian. I believe him to be the protector of his master's honor, or, let us say, of his master's property, whether that property be silver plate or the woman his master loves. Last night, after Lord Arthur had gone away, the servant was left alone in this house with Lord Chetney and Madame Zichy. From where he sat in the hall he could hear Lord Chetney bidding her farewell; for, if my idea of him is correct, he understands English quite as well as you or I. Let us imagine that he heard her entreating Chetney not to leave her, reminding him of his former wish to marry her, and let us suppose that he hears Chetney denounce her, and tell her that at Cairo he has learned of this Russian admirer—the servant's master. He hears the woman declare that she has had no admirer but himself, that this unknown Russian was, and is, nothing to her, that there is no man she loves but him, and that she cannot live, knowing that he is alive, without his love. Suppose Chetney believed her, suppose his former infatuation for her returned, and that in a moment of weakness he forgave her and took her in his arms. That is the moment the Russian master has feared. It is to guard against it that he has placed his watchdog over the Princess, and how do we know but that, when the moment came, the watchdog served his master, as he saw his duty, and killed them both? What do you think?' Lyle demanded. 'Would not that explain both murders?'

"I was only too willing to hear any theory which pointed to any one else as the criminal than Arthur, but Lyle's explanation was too utterly fantastic. I told him that he certainly showed imagination, but that he could not hang a man for what he imagined he had done.

"'No,' Lyle answered, 'but I can frighten him by telling him what I think he

has done, and now when I again question the Russian servant I will make it quite clear to him that I believe he is the murderer. I think that will open his mouth. A man will at least talk to defend himself. Come,' he said, 'we must return at once to Scotland Yard and see him. There is nothing more to do here.'

"He arose, and I followed him into the hall, and in another minute we would have been on our way to Scotland Yard. But just as he opened the street door a postman halted at the gate of the garden, and began fumbling with the latch.

"Lyle stopped, with an exclamation of chagrin.

"'How stupid of me!' he exclaimed. He turned quickly and pointed to a narrow slit cut in the brass plate of the front door. 'The house has a private letter-box,' he said, 'and I had not thought to look in it! If we had gone out as we came in, by the window, I would never have seen it. The moment I entered the house I should have thought of securing the letters which came this morning. I have been grossly careless.' He stepped back into the hall and pulled at the lid of the letterbox, which hung on the inside of the door, but it was tightly locked. At the same moment the postman came up the steps holding a letter. Without a word Lyle took it from his hand and began to examine it. It was addressed to the Princess Zichy, and on the back of the envelope was the name of a West End dressmaker.

"'That is of no use to me,' Lyle said. He took out his card and showed it to the postman. 'I am Inspector Lyle from Scotland Yard,' he said. 'The people in this house are under arrest. Everything it contains is now in my keeping. Did you deliver any other letters here this morning!'

"The man looked frightened, but answered promptly that he was now upon his third round. He had made one postal delivery at seven that morning and another at eleven.

"'How many letters did you leave here!' Lyle asked.

"'About six altogether,' the man answered.

"'Did you put them through the door into the letter-box!'

"The postman said, 'Yes, I always slip them into the box, and ring and go away. The servants collect them from the inside.'

"'Have you noticed if any of the letters you leave here bear a Russian postage stamp!' Lyle asked.

"The man answered, 'Oh, yes, sir, a great many.'

"'From the same person, would you say!'

"'The writing seems to be the same,' the man answered. 'They come regularly about once a week—one of those I delivered this morning had a Russian postmark.'

"'That will do,' said Lyle eagerly. 'Thank you, thank you very much.'

"He ran back into the hall, and, pulling out his penknife, began to pick at the lock of the letter-box.

"'I have been supremely careless,' he said in great excitement. 'Twice before when people I wanted had flown from a house I have been able to follow them by putting a guard over their mail-box. These letters, which arrive regularly every week from Russia in the same handwriting, they can come but from one person. At least, we shall now know the name of the master of this house. Undoubtedly it is one of his letters that the man placed here this morning. We may make a most important discovery.'

"As he was talking he was picking at the lock with his knife, but he was so impatient to reach the letters that he pressed too heavily on the blade and it broke in his hand. I took a step backward and drove my heel into the lock, and burst it open. The lid flew back, and we pressed forward, and each ran his hand down into the letterbox. For a moment we were both too startled to move. The box was empty.

"I do not know how long we stood staring stupidly at each other, but it was Lyle who was the first to recover. He seized me by the arm and pointed excitedly into the empty box.

"'Do you appreciate what that means?' he cried. 'It means that some one has been here ahead of us. Some one has entered this house not three hours before we came, since eleven o'clock this morning.'

"'It was the Russian servant!' I exclaimed.

"'The Russian servant has been under arrest at Scotland Yard,' Lyle cried. 'He could not have taken the letters. Lord Arthur has been in his cot at the hospital. That is his alibi. There is some one else, some one we do not suspect, and that some one is the murderer. He came back here either to obtain those letters because he knew they would convict him, or to remove something he had left here at the time of the murder, something incriminating,—the weapon, perhaps, or some personal article; a cigarette-case, a handkerchief with his name upon it, or a pair of gloves. Whatever it was it must have been damning evidence against him to have made him take so desperate a chance.'

"'How do we know,' I whispered, 'that he is not hidden here now?'

"'No, I'll swear he is not,' Lyle answered. 'I may have bungled in some things, but I have searched this house thoroughly. Nevertheless,' he added, 'we must go over it again, from the cellar to the roof. We have the real clew now, and we must forget the others and work only it.' As he spoke he began again to search the drawing-room, turning over even the books on the tables and the music on the piano. "'Whoever the man is,' he said over his shoulder, 'we know that he has a key to the front door and a key to the letter-box. That shows us he is either an inmate of the house or that he comes here when he wishes. The Russian says that he was the only servant in the house. Certainly we have found no evidence to show that any other servant slept here. There could be but one other person who would possess a key to the house and the letter-box—and he lives in St. Petersburg. At the time of the murder he was two thousand miles away.' Lyle interrupted himself suddenly with a sharp cry and turned upon me with his eyes flashing. 'But was he?' he cried. 'Was he? How do we know that last night he was not in London, in this very house when Zichy and Chetney met?'

"He stood staring at me without seeing me, muttering, and arguing with himself.

"'Don't speak to me,' he cried, as I ventured to interrupt him. 'I can see it now. It is all plain. It was not the servant, but his master, the Russian himself, and it was he who came back for the letters! He came back for them because he knew they would convict him. We must find them. We must have those letters. If we find the one with the Russian postmark, we shall have found the murderer.' He spoke like a madman, and as he spoke he ran around the room with one hand held out in front of him as you have seen a mind-reader at a theatre seeking for something hidden in the stalls. He pulled the old letters from the writing-desk, and ran them over as swiftly as a gambler deals out cards; he dropped on his knees before the fireplace and dragged out the dead coals with his bare fingers, and then with a low, worried cry, like a hound on a scent, he ran back to the waste-paper basket and, lifting the papers from it, shook them out upon the floor. Instantly he gave a shout of triumph, and, separating a number of torn pieces from the others, held them up before me.

"'Look!' he cried. 'Do you see? Here are five letters, torn across in two places. The Russian did not stop to read them, for, as you see, he has left them still sealed. I have been wrong. He did not return for the letters. He could not have known their value. He must have returned for some other reason, and, as he was leaving, saw the letter-box, and taking out the letters, held them together—so—and tore them twice across, and then, as the fire had gone out, tossed them into this basket. Look!' he cried, 'here in the upper corner of this piece is a Russian stamp. This is his own letter—unopened!'

"We examined the Russian stamp and found it had been cancelled in St. Petersburg four days ago. The back of the envelope bore the postmark of the branch station in upper Sloane Street, and was dated this morning. The envelope was of official blue paper and we had no difficulty in finding the two other parts of it. We drew the torn pieces of the letter from them and joined them together side by side. There were but two lines of writing, and this was the message: 'I leave Petersburg on the night train, and I shall see you at Trevor Terrace after dinner Monday evening.'

"'That was last night!' Lyle cried. 'He arrived twelve hours ahead of his letter—but it came in time—it came in time to hang him!'"

The Baronet struck the table with his hand.

"The name!" he demanded. "How was it signed? What was the man's name!"

The young Solicitor rose to his feet and, leaning forward, stretched out his arm. "There was no name," he cried. "The letter was signed with only two initials. But engraved at the top of the sheet was the man's address. That address was 'THE AMERICAN EMBASSY, ST. PETERSBURG, BUREAU or THE NAVAL ATTACHE,' and the initials," he shouted, his voice rising into an exultant and bitter cry, "were those of the gentleman who sits opposite who told us that he was the first to find the murdered bodies, the Naval Attache to Russia, Lieutenant Sears!"

A strained and awful hush followed the Solicitor's words, which seemed to vibrate like a twanging bowstring that had just hurled its bolt. Sir Andrew, pale and staring, drew away with an exclamation of repulsion. His eyes were fastened upon the Naval Attache with fascinated horror. But the American emitted a sigh of great content, and sank comfortably into the arms of his chair. He clapped his hands softly together.

"Capital!" he murmured. "I give you my word I never guessed what you were driving at. You fooled *me,* I'll be hanged if you didn't—you certainly fooled me."

The man with the pearl stud leaned forward with a nervous gesture. "Hush! be careful!" he whispered. But at that instant, for the third time, a servant, hastening through the room, handed him a piece of paper which he scanned eagerly. The message on the paper read, "The light over the Commons is out. The House has risen."

The man with the black pearl gave a mighty shout, and tossed the paper from him upon the table.

"Hurrah!" he cried. "The House is up! We've won!" He caught up his glass, and slapped the Naval Attache violently upon the shoulder. He nodded joyously at him, at the Solicitor, and at the Queen's Messenger. "Gentlemen, to you!" he cried; "my thanks and my congratulations!" He drank deep from the glass, and breathed forth a long sigh of satisfaction and relief.

"But I say," protested the Queen's Messenger, shaking his finger violently at the Solicitor, "that story won't do. You didn't play fair—and—and you talked so fast I couldn't make out what it was all about. I'll bet you that evidence wouldn't hold in a court of law—you couldn't hang a cat on such evidence. Your story is condemned tommy-rot. Now my story might have happened, my story bore the mark—"

In the joy of creation the story-tellers had forgotten their audience, until a sudden exclamation from Sir Andrew caused them to turn guiltily toward him. His face was knit with lines of anger, doubt, and amazement.

"What does this mean!" he cried. "Is this a jest, or are you mad? If you know this man is a murderer, why is he at large? Is this a game you have been playing? Explain yourselves at once. What does it mean?"

The American, with first a glance at the others, rose and bowed courteously.

"I am not a murderer, Sir Andrew, believe me," he said; "you need not be alarmed. As a matter of fact, at this moment I am much more afraid of you than you could possibly be of me. I beg you please to be indulgent. I assure you, we meant no disrespect. We have been matching stories, that is all, pretending that we are people we are not, endeavoring to entertain you with better detective tales than, for instance, the last one you read, 'The Great Rand Robbery.'"

The Baronet brushed his hand nervously across his forehead.

"Do you mean to tell me," he exclaimed, "that none of this has happened? That Lord Chetney is not dead, that his Solicitor did not find a letter of yours written from your post in Petersburg, and that just now, when he charged you with murder, he was in jest?"

"I am really very sorry," said the American, "but you see, sir, he could not have found a letter written by me in St. Petersburg because I have never been in Petersburg. Until this week, I have never been outside of my own country. I am not a naval officer. I am a writer of short stories. And tonight, when this gentleman told me that you were fond of detective stories, I thought it would be amusing to tell you one of my own—one I had just mapped out this afternoon."

"But Lord Chetney *is* a real person," interrupted the Baronet, "and he did go to Africa two years ago, and he was supposed to have died there, and his brother, Lord Arthur, has been the heir. And yesterday Chetney did return. I read it in the papers." "So did I," assented the American soothingly; "and it struck me as being a very good plot for a story. I mean his unexpected return from the dead, and the probable disappointment of the younger brother. So I decided that the younger brother had better murder the older one. The Princess Zichy I invented out of a clear sky. The fog I did not have to invent. Since last night I know all that there is to know about a London fog. I was lost in one for three hours."

The Baronet turned grimly upon the Queen's Messenger.

"But this gentleman," he protested, "he is not a writer of short stories; he is a member of the Foreign Office. I have often seen him in Whitehall, and, according to him, the Princess Zichy is not an invention. He says she is very well known, that she tried to rob him."

The servant of the Foreign Office looked unhappily at the Cabinet Minister, and puffed nervously on his cigar.

"It's true, Sir Andrew, that I am a Queen's Messenger," he said appealingly, "and a Russian woman once did try to rob a Queen's Messenger in a railway carriage—only it did not happen to me, but to a pal of mine. The only Russian princess I ever knew called herself Zabrisky. You may have seen her. She used to do a dive from the roof of the Aquarium."

Sir Andrew, with a snort of indignation, fronted the young Solicitor.

"And I suppose yours was a cock-and-bull story, too," he said. "Of course, it must have been, since Lord Chetney is not dead. But don't tell me," he protested, "that you are not Chudleigh's son either."

"I'm sorry," said the youngest member, smiling in some embarrassment, "but my name is not Chudleigh. I assure you, though, that I know the family very well, and that I am on very good terms with them."

"You should be!" exclaimed the Baronet; "and, judging from the liberties you take with the Chetneys, you had better be on very good terms with them, too."

The young man leaned back and glanced toward the servants at the far end of the room.

"It has been so long since I have been in the Club," he said, "that I doubt if even the waiters remember me. Perhaps Joseph may," he added. "Joseph!" he called, and at the word a servant stepped briskly forward.

The young man pointed to the stuffed head of a great lion which was suspended above the fireplace.

"Joseph," he said, "I want you to tell these gentlemen who shot that lion. Who presented it to the Grill?"

Joseph, unused to acting as master of ceremonies to members of the Club, shifted nervously from one foot to the other.

"Why, you—you did," he stammered.

"Of course I did!" exclaimed the young man. "I mean, what is the name of the man who shot it! Tell the gentlemen who I am. They wouldn't believe me."

"Who you are, my lord?" said Joseph. "You are Lord Edam's son, the Earl of Chetney."

"You must admit," said Lord Chetney, when the noise had died away, "that I couldn't remain dead while my little brother was accused of murder. I had to do something. Family pride demanded it. Now, Arthur, as the younger brother, can't afford to be squeamish, but personally I should hate to have a brother of mine hanged for murder."

"You certainly showed no scruples against hanging me," said the American, "but in the face of your evidence I admit my guilt, and I sentence myself to pay the full penalty of the law as we are made to pay it in my own country. The order of this court is," he announced, "that Joseph shall bring me a wine-card, and that I sign it for five bottles of the Club's best champagne." "Oh, no!" protested the man with the pearl stud, "it is not for *you* to sign it. In my opinion it is Sir Andrew who should pay the costs. It is time you knew," he said, turning to that gentleman, "that unconsciously you have been the victim of what I may call a patriotic conspiracy. These stories have had a more serious purpose than merely to amuse. They have been told with the worthy object of detaining you from the House of Commons. I must explain to you, that all through this evening I have had a servant waiting in Trafalgar Square with instructions to bring me word as soon as the light over the House of Commons had ceased to burn. The light is now out, and the object for which we plotted is attained."

The Baronet glanced keenly at the man with the black pearl, and then quickly at his watch. The smile disappeared from his lips, and his face was set in stern and forbidding lines.

"And may I know," he asked icily, "what was the object of your plot!"

"A most worthy one," the other retorted. "Our object was to keep you from advocating the expenditure of many millions of the people's money upon more battleships. In a word, we have been working together to prevent you from passing the Navy Increase Bill."

Sir Andrew's face bloomed with brilliant color. His body shook with suppressed emotion.

"My dear sir!" he cried, "you should spend more time at the House and less at your Club. The Navy Bill was brought up on its third reading at eight o'clock this evening. I spoke for three hours in its favor. My only reason for wishing to return again to the House to-night was to sup on the terrace with my old friend, Admiral Simons; for my work at the House was completed five hours ago, when the Navy Increase Bill was passed by an overwhelming majority."

The Baronet rose and bowed. "I have to thank you, sir," he said, "for a most interesting evening."

The American shoved the wine-card which Joseph had given him toward the gentleman with the black pearl.

"You sign it," he said.

Hearts and Masks
By Harold MacGrath

Originally Published in 1905

HEARTS AND MASKS
BY HAROLD MACGRATH

Mistaken identity at a masked ball is a device as old as the theatre, and as cover for a jewel thief, it has a history nearly as long. Yet in this tale of two young lovers who crash such a ball, MacGrath weaves a story that is both mysterious and romantic. They find themselves caught up in a daring robbery when the young man accidentally happens to choose the same costume as the thief. And that is only the first case of assumed confused identities. But this story is really more about love than crime.

About the Author

Harold MacGrath (September 4, 1871-October 30, 1930) was an American novelist and writer of screenplays. Born in Syracuse, New York, he first worked as a journalist for the Syracuse Herald before turning to fiction. He wrote stories and novels of romance, mystery, espionage, and adventure, and in addition to having a number of top ten selling books he also wrote stories for many of the major magazines of the day. He was one of the first major authors to write for the film industry and over twenty of his stories and novels were turned into films.

HEARTS AND MASKS

I

It all depends upon the manner of your entrance to the Castle of Adventure. One does not have to scale its beetling parapets or assault its scarps and frowning bastions; neither is one obliged to force with clamor and blaring trumpets and glittering gorgets the drawbridge and portcullis. Rather the pathway lies through one of those many little doors, obscure, yet easily accessible, latchless and boltless, to which the average person gives no particular attention, and yet which invariably lead to the very heart of this Castle Delectable. The whimsical chatelaine of this enchanted keep is a shy goddess. Circumspection has no part in her affairs, nor caution, nor practicality; nor does her eye linger upon the dullard and the blunderer. Imagination solves the secret riddle, and wit is the guide that leads the seeker through the winding, bewildering labyrinths.

And there is something in being idle, too!

If I had not gone idly into Mouquin's cellar for dinner that night, I should have missed the most engaging adventure that ever fell to my lot. It is second nature for me to be guided by impulse rather than by reason; reason is always so square-toed and impulse is always so alluring. You will find that nearly all the great captains were and are creatures of impulse; nothing brilliant is ever achieved by calculation. All this is not to say that I am a great captain; it is offered only to inform you that I am often impulsive.

A *Times*, four days old; and if I hadn't fallen upon it to pass the twenty-odd minutes between my order and the service of it, I shouldn't have made the acquaintance of the police in that pretty little suburb over in New Jersey; nor should I have met the enchanting Blue Domino; nor would fate have written Kismet. The clairvoyant never has any fun in this cycle; he has no surprises.

I had been away from New York for several weeks, and had returned only that afternoon. Thus, the spirit of unrest acquired by travel was still upon me. It was nearing holiday week, and those congenial friends I might have called upon, to while away the evening, were either busily occupied with shopping or were out of town; and I determined not to go to the club and be bored by some indifferent billiard player. I would dine quietly, listen to some light music, and then go to the theater. I was searching the theatrical amusements, when the society column indifferently attacked my eye. I do not know why it is, but I have a wholesome contempt for the so-called society columns of the daily newspaper in New York. Mayhap, it is because I do not belong.

I read this paragraph with a shrug, and that one with a smirk. I was in no manner surprised at the announcement that Miss High-Culture was going to wed the Duke of Impecune; I had always been certain this girl would do some such fool thing. That Mrs. Hyphen-Bonds was giving a farewell dinner at the Waldorf, prior to her departure to Europe, interested my curiosity not in the least degree. It would be all the same to me if she never came back. None of the wishy-washy tittle-tattle interested me, in fact. There was only one little six-line paragraph that really caught me. On Friday night (that is to say, the night of my adventures in Blankshire), the Hunt Club was to give a charity masquerade dance. This grasped my adventurous spirit by the throat and refused to let go.

The atmosphere surrounding the paragraph was spirituous with enchantment. There was a genuine novelty about this dance. Two packs of playing-cards had been sent out as tickets; one pack to the ladies and one to the gentlemen. Charming idea, wasn't it? These cards were to be shown at the door, together with ten dollars, but were to be retained by the recipients till two o'clock (supper-time), at which moment everybody was to unmask and take his partner, who held the corresponding card, in to supper. Its newness strongly appealed to me. I found myself reading the paragraph over and over.

By Jove, what an inspiration!

I knew the Blankshire Hunt Club, with its colonial architecture, its great ball-room, its quaint fireplaces, its stables and sheds, and the fame of its chef. It was one of those great country clubs that keep open house the year round. It stood back from the sea about four miles and was within five miles of the village. There was a fine course inland, a cross-country going of not less than twenty miles, a shooting-box, and excellent golf-links. In the winter it was cozy; in the summer it was ideal.

I was intimately acquainted with the club's M. F. H., Teddy Hamilton. We had done the Paris-Berlin run in my racing-car the summer before. If I hadn't known him so well, I might still have been in durance vile, next door to jail, or securely inside. I had frequently dined with him at the club during the summer, and he had offered to put me up; but as I knew no one intimately but himself, I explained the futility of such action. Besides, my horse wasn't a hunter; and I was riding him less and less. It is no pleasure to go "parking" along the bridle-paths of Central Park. For myself, I want a hill country and something like forty miles, straight away; that's riding.

The fact that I knew no one but Teddy added zest to the inspiration which had seized me. For I determined to attend that dance, happen what might. It would be vastly more entertaining than a possibly dull theatrical performance. (It was!)

I called for a messenger and despatched him to the nearest drug store for a pack of playing-cards; and while I waited for his return I casually glanced at the other diners. At my table—one of those long marble-topped affairs by the wall—there was an old man reading a paper, and the handsomest girl I had set eyes upon in a month of moons. Sometimes the word handsome seems an inferior adjective. She was beautiful, and her half-lidded eyes told me that she was anywhere but at Mouquin's. What a head of hair! Fine as a spider's web, and the dazzling yellow of a wheat-field in a sun-shower! The irregularity of her features made them all the more interesting. I was an artist in an amateur way, and I mentally painted in that head against a Rubens background. The return of the messenger brought me back to earth; for I confess that my imagination had already leaped far into the future, and this girl across the way was nebulously connected with it.

I took the pack of cards, ripped off the covering, tossed aside the joker (though, really, I ought to have retained it!) and began shuffling the shiny pasteboards. I dare say that those around

me sat up and took notice. It was by no means a common sight
to see a man gravely shuffling a pack of cards in a public
restaurant. Nobody interfered, doubtless because nobody knew
exactly what to do in the face of such an act, for which no
adequate laws had been provided. A waiter stood solemnly at
the end of the table, scratching his chin thoughtfully, wondering
whether he should report this peculiarity of constitution and
susceptibility occasioning certain peculiarities of effect from
impress of extraneous influences (*vide* Webster), synonymous
with idiocrasy and known as idiosyncrasy. It was quite possible
that I was the first man to establish such a precedent in
Monsieur Mouquin's restaurant. Thus, I aroused only passive
curiosity.

From the corner of my eye I observed the old gentleman
opposite. He was peering over the top of his paper, and I could
see by the glitter in his eye that he was a confirmed player of
solitaire. The girl, however, still appeared to be in a dreaming
state. I have no doubt every one who saw me thought that
anarchy was abroad again, or that Sherlock Holmes had entered
into his third incarnation.

Finally I squared the pack, took a long-breath, and cut. I
turned up the card. It was the ten-spot of hearts. I considered
this most propitious; hearts being my long suit in everything but
love,—love having not yet crossed my path. I put the card in my
wallet, and was about to toss the rest of the pack under the
table, when, a woman's voice stayed my hand.

"Don't throw them away. Tell my fortune first."

I looked up, not a little surprised. It was the beautiful young
girl who had spoken. She was leaning on her elbows, her chin
propped in her palms, and the light in her grey *chatoyant* eyes
was wholly innocent and mischievous. In Monsieur Mouquin's
cellar people are rather Bohemian, not to say friendly; for it is
the rendezvous of artists, literary men and journalists,—a clan
that holds formality in contempt.

"Tell your fortune?" I repeated parrot-like.

"Yes."

"Your mirror can tell you that more accurately than I can," I
replied with a frank glance of admiration.

She drew her shoulders together and dropped them. "I spoke
to you, sir, because I believed you wouldn't say anything so

commonplace as that. When one sees a man soberly shuffling a pack of cards in a place like this, one naturally expects originality."

"Well, perhaps you caught me off my guard,"—humbly.

"I am original. Did you ever before witness this performance in a public restaurant?"—making the cards purr.

"I can not say I have,"—amused.

"Well, no more have I!"

"Why, then, do you do it?"—with renewed interest.

"Shall I tell your fortune?"

"Not now. I had much rather you would tell me the meaning of this play."

I leaned toward her and whispered mysteriously: "The truth is, I belong to a secret society, and I was cutting the cards to see whether or not I should blow up the post-office to-night or the police-station. You mustn't tell anybody."

"Oh!" She started back from the table. "You do not look it," she added suddenly.

"I know it; appearances are so deceptive," said I sadly.

Then the old man laughed, and the girl laughed, and I laughed; and I wasn't quite sure that the grave waiter did not crack the ghost of a smile—in relief.

"And what, may I ask, was the fatal card?" inquired the old man, folding his paper.

"The ace of spades; we always choose that gloomy card in secret societies. There is something deadly and suggestive about it," I answered morbidly.

"Indeed."

"Yes. Ah, if only you knew the terrible life we lead, we who conspire! Every day brings forth some galling disappointment. We push a king off into the dark, and another rises immediately in his place. Futility, futility everywhere! If only there were some way of dynamiting habit and custom! I am a Russian; all my family are perishing in Siberian mines,"—dismally.

"Fudge!" said the girl.

"Tommy-rot!" said the amiable old gentleman.

"Uncle, his hair is too short for an anarchist."

"And his collar too immaculate." (So the old gentleman was this charming creature's uncle!)

"We are obliged to disguise ourselves at times," I explained. "The police are always meddling. It is discouraging."

"You have some purpose, humorous or serious," said the girl shrewdly. "A man does not bring a pack of cards—"

"I didn't bring them; I sent out for them."

"—bring a pack of cards here simply to attract attention," she continued tranquilly.

"Perhaps I am a prestidigitator in a popular dime-museum," I suggested, willing to help her out, "and am doing a little advertising."

"Now, that has a plausible sound," she admitted, folding her hands under her chin. "It must be an interesting life. *Presto— change*! and all that."

"Oh, I find it rather monotonous in the winter; but in the summer it is fine. Then I wander about the summer resorts and give exhibitions."

"You will pardon my niece," interpolated the old gentleman, coughing a bit nervously. "If she annoys you—"

"Uncle!"—reproachfully.

"Heaven forfend!" I exclaimed eagerly. "There is a charm in doing unconventional things; and most people do not realize it, and are stupid."

"Thank you, sir," said the girl, smiling. She was evidently enjoying herself; so was I, for that matter. "Do a trick for me," she commanded presently.

I smiled weakly. I couldn't have done a trick with the cards,—not if my life had depended upon it. But I rather neatly extricated myself from the trap.

"I never do any tricks out of business hours."

"Uncle, give the gentleman ten cents; I want to see him do a sleight-of-hand trick."

Her uncle, readily entering into the spirit of the affair, dived into a pocket and produced the piece of silver. It looked as if I were caught.

"There! this may make it worth your while," the girl said, shoving the coin in my direction.

But again I managed to slide under; I was not to be caught.

"It is my regret to say,"—frowning slightly, "that regularity in my business is everything. It wants half an hour for my turn to come on. If I tried a trick out of turn, I might foozle and lose prestige. And besides, I depend so much upon the professor and his introductory notes: 'Ladies and gents, permit me to introduce the world-renowned Signor Fantoccini, whose marvelous tricks have long puzzled all the crowned heads of Europe—'"

"Fantoccini,"—musingly. "That's Italian for puppet show."

"I know it, but the dime-museum visitors do not. It makes a fine impression."

She laughed and slid the dime back to her uncle.

"I'm afraid you are an impostor," she said.

"I'm afraid so, too," I confessed, laughing.

Then the comedy came to an end by the appearance of our separate orders. I threw aside the cards and proceeded to attack my dinner, for I was hungry. From time to time I caught vague fragments of conversation between the girl and her uncle.

"It's a fool idea," mumbled the old gentleman; "you will get into some trouble or other."

"That doesn't matter. It will be like a vacation,—a flash of old Rome, where I wish I were at this very moment. I am determined."

"This is what comes of reading romantic novels,"—with a kind of grumble.

"I admit there never was a particle of romance on your side of the family," the girl retorted.

"Happily. There is peace in the house where I live."

"Do not argue with me."

"I am not arguing with you. I should only be wasting my time. I am simply warning you that you are about to commit a folly."

"I have made up my mind."

"Ah! In that case I have hopes," he returned. "When a woman makes up her mind to do one thing, she generally does another. Why can't you put aside this fool idea and go to the opera with me?"

"I have seen *Carmen* in Paris, Rome, London and New York," she replied.

(Evidently a traveled young person.)

"*Carmen* is your favorite opera, besides."

"Not to-night,"—whimsically.

"Go, then; but please recollect that if anything serious comes of your folly, I did my best to prevent it. It's a scatter-brained idea, and no good will come of it, mark me."

"I can take care of myself,"—truculently.

"So I have often been forced to observe,"—dryly.

(I wondered what it was all about.)

"But, uncle dear, I am becoming so dreadfully bored!"

"That sounds final," sighed the old man, helping himself to the *haricots verts*. (The girl ate positively nothing.) "But it seems odd that you can't go about your affairs after my own reasonable manner."

"I am only twenty."

The old man's shoulders rose and fell resignedly.

"No man has an answer for that."

"I promise to tell you everything that happens; by telegraph."

"That's small comfort. Imagine receiving a telegram early in the morning, when a man's brain is without invention or coherency of thought! I would that you were back home with your father. I might sleep o' nights, then."

"I have so little amusement!"

"You work three hours a day and earn more in a week than your father and I do in a month. Yours is a very unhappy lot."

"I hate the smell of paints; I hate the studio."

"And I suppose you hate your fame?" acridly.

"Bah! that is my card to a living. The people I meet bore me."

"Not satisfied with common folks, eh? Must have kings and queens to talk to?"

"I only want to live abroad, and you and father will not let me,"—petulantly.

The music started up, and I heard no more. Occasionally the girl glanced at me and smiled in a friendly fashion. She was evidently an artist's model; and when they have hair and color like this girl's, the pay is good. I found myself wondering why she was bored and why Carmen had so suddenly lost its charms.

It was seven o'clock when I pushed aside my plate and paid my check. I calculated that by hustling I could reach Blankshire either at ten or ten-thirty. That would be early enough for my needs. And now to route out a costumer. All I needed was a grey mask. I had in my apartments a Capuchin's robe and cowl. I rose, lighting a cigarette.

The girl looked up from her coffee.

"Back to the dime-museum?"—banteringly.

"I have a few minutes to spare," said I.

"By the way, I forgot to ask you what card you drew."

"It was the ten of hearts."

"The ten of hearts?" Her amazement was not understandable.

"Yes, the ten of hearts; Cupid and all that."

She recovered her composure quickly.

"Then you will not blow up the post-office to-night?"

"No," I replied, "not to-night."

"You have really and truly aroused my curiosity. Tell me, what does the ten of hearts mean to you?"

I gazed thoughtfully down at her. Had I truly mystified her? There was some doubt in my mind.

"Frankly, I wish I might tell you. All I am at liberty to say is that I am about to set forth upon a desperate adventure, and I shall be very fortunate if I do not spend the night in the lock-up."

"You do not look desperate."

"Oh, I am not desperate; it is only the adventure that is desperate."

"Some princess in durance vile? Some villain to smite? Citadels to storm?" Her smile was enchantment itself.

I hesitated a moment. "What would you say if I told you that this adventure was merely to prove to myself what a consummate ass the average man can be upon occasions?"

"Why go to the trouble of proving it?"—drolly.

"I am conceited enough to have some doubts as to the degree."

"Consider it positive."

I laughed. "I am in hopes that I am neither a positive ass nor a superlative one, only comparative."

"But the adventure; that is the thing that mainly interests me."

"Oh, that is a secret which I should hesitate to tell even to the Sphinx."

"I see you are determined not to illuminate the darkness,"—and she turned carelessly toward her uncle, who was serenely contemplating the glowing end of a fat perfecto.

I bowed and passed out in Sixth Avenue, rather regretting that I had not the pleasure of the charming young person's acquaintance.

The ten-spot of hearts seemed to have startled her for some reason. I wondered why.

The snow blew about me, whirled, and swirled, and stung. Oddly enough I recalled the paragraph relative to Mrs. Hyphen-Bonds. By this time she was being very well tossed about in mid-ocean. As the old order of yarn-spinners used to say, little did I dream what was in store for me, or the influence the magic name of Hyphen-Bonds was to have upon my destiny.

Bismillah! (Whatever that means!)

II

After half an hour's wandering about I stumbled across a curio-shop, a weird, dim and dusty, musty old curio-shop, with stuffed peacocks hanging from the ceiling, and skulls, and bronzes and marbles, paintings, tarnished jewelry and ancient armor, rare books in vellum, small arms, tapestry, pastimes, plaster masks, and musical instruments. I recalled to mind the shop of the dealer in antiquities in Balzac's *La Peau de Chagrin*, and glanced about (not without a shiver) for the fatal ass's skin. (I forgot that I was wearing it myself that night!) I was something of a collector of antiquities, of the inanimate kind, and for a time I became lost in speculation,—speculation rather agreeable of its kind, I liked to conjure up in fancy the various scenes through which these curiosities had drifted in their descent to this demi-pawnshop; the brave men and beautiful women, the clangor of tocsins, the haze of battles, the glitter of ball-rooms, epochs and ages. What romance lay behind yon satin slipper? What *grande dame* had smiled behind that ivory fan? What meant that tarnished silver mask?

The old French proprietor was evidently all things from a pawnbroker to an art collector; for most of the jewelry was in excellent order and the pictures possessed value far beyond the intrinsic. He was waiting upon a customer, and the dingy light that shone down on his bald bumpy head made it look for all the world like an ill-used billiard-ball. He was exhibiting revolvers.

From the shining metal of the small arms, my glance traveled to the face of the prospective buyer. It was an interesting face, clean-cut, beardless, energetic, but the mouth impressed me as being rather hard. Doubtless he felt the magnetism of my scrutiny, for he suddenly looked around. The expression on his face was not one to induce me to throw my arms around his neck and declare I should be glad to make his acquaintance. It was a scowl. He was in evening dress, and I could see that he knew very well how to wear it. All this was but momentary. He took up a revolver and balanced it on his palm.

By and by the proprietor came sidling along behind the cases, the slip-slip fashion of his approach informing me that he wore slippers.

"Do you keep costumes?" I asked.

"Anything you like, sir, from a crusader to a modern gentleman,"—with grim and appropriate irony. "What is it you are in search of—a masquerade costume?'"

"Only a grey mask," I answered. "I am going to a masked ball to-night as a Grey Capuchin, and I want a mask that will match my robe."

"Your wants are simple."

From a shelf he brought down a box, took off the cover, and left me to make my selection. Soon I found what I desired and laid it aside, waiting for Monsieur Friard to return. Again I observed the other customer. There is always a mystery to be solved and a story to be told, when a man makes the purchase of a pistol in a pawnshop. A man who buys a pistol for the sake of protection does so in the light of day, and in the proper place, a

gun-shop. He does not haunt the pawnbroker in the dusk of evening. Well, it was none of my business; doubtless he knew what he was doing. I coughed suggestively, and Friard came slipping in my direction again.

"This is what I want. How much?" I inquired.

"Fifty cents; it has never been worn."

I drew out my wallet. I had arrived in town too late to go to the bank, and I was carrying an uncomfortably large sum in gold-bills. As I opened the wallet to extract a small bill, I saw the stranger eying me quietly. Well, well, the dullest being brightens at the sight of money and its representatives. I drew out a small bill and handed it to the proprietor. He took it, together with the mask, and sidled over to the cash-register. The bell gave forth a muffled sound, not unlike that of a fire-bell in a snow-storm. As he was in the act of wrapping up my purchase, I observed the silent customer's approach. When he reached my side he stooped and picked up something from the floor. With a bow he presented it to me.

"I saw it drop from your pocket," he said; and then when he saw what it was, his jaw fell, and he sent me a hot, penetrating glance.

"The ten of hearts!" he exclaimed in amazement.

I laughed easily.

"The ten of hearts!" he repeated.

"Yes; four hearts on one side and four on the other, and two in the middle, which make ten in all,"—raillery in my tones. What the deuce *was* the matter with everybody to-night? "Marvelous card, isn't it?"

"Very strange!" he murmured, pulling at his lips.

"And in what way is it strange?" I asked, rather curious to learn the cause of his agitation.

"There are several reasons,"—briefly.

"Ah!"

"I have seen a man's hand pinned to that card; therefore it is gruesome."

"Some card-sharper?"

He nodded. "Then again, I lost a small fortune because of that card,"—diffidently.

"Poker?"

"Yes. Why will a man try to fill a royal flush? The man next to me drew the ten of hearts, the very card I needed. The sight of it always unnerves me. I beg your pardon."

"Oh, that's all right," said I, wondering how many more lies he had up his sleeve.

"And there's still another reason. I saw a man put six bullets into the two central spots, and an hour later the seventh bullet snuffed the candle of a friend of mine. I am from the West."

"I can sympathize with you," I returned. "After all that trouble, the sight of the card must have given you a shock."

Then I stowed away the fatal card and took up my bundle and change. I have in my own time tried to fill royal flushes, and the disappointment still lingers with a bitter taste.

"The element of chance is the most fascinating thing there is," the stranger from the West volunteered.

"So it is," I replied, suddenly recalling that I was soon to put my trust in the hands of that very fickle goddess.

He nodded and returned to his revolvers, while I went out of the shop, hailed a cab, and drove up-town to my apartments in Riverside. It was eight o'clock by my watch. I leaned back against the cushions, ruminating. There seemed to be something going on that night; the ten of hearts was acquiring a mystifying, not to say sinister, aspect. First it had alarmed the girl in Mouquin's, and now this stranger in the curio-shop. I was confident that the latter had lied in regard to his explanations. The card *had* startled him, but his reasons were altogether of transparent thinness. A man never likes to confess that he is unlucky at cards; there is a certain pride in lying about the enormous stakes you have won and the wonderful draws you have made. I frowned. It was not possible for me to figure out what his interest in the card was. If he was a Westerner, his buying a pistol in a pawnshop was at once disrobed of its mystery; but the inconsistent elegance of his evening clothes doubled my suspicions. Bah! What was the use of troubling myself with this stranger's affairs? He would never cross my path again.

In reasonable time the cab drew up in front of my apartments. I dressed, donned my Capuchin's robe and took a look at myself in the pier-glass. Then I unwrapped the package and put on the mask. The whole made a capital outfit, and I was vastly pleased with myself. This was going to be such an adventure as one reads about in the ancient numbers of *Blackwood's*. I slipped the robe and mask into my suit-case and lighted my pipe. During great moments like this, a man gathers courage and confidence from a pipeful of tobacco. I dropped into a comfortable Morris, touched the gas-logs, and fell into a pleasant dream. It was not necessary for me to start for the Twenty-third Street ferry till nine; so I had something like three-quarters of an hour to idle away. . . . What beautiful hair that girl had! It was like sunshine, the silk of corn, the yield of the harvest. And the marvelous abundance of it! It was true that she was an artist's model; it was equally true that she had committed a mild impropriety in addressing me as she had; but, for all I could see, she was a girl of delicate breeding, doubtless one of the many whose family fortunes, or misfortunes, force them to earn a living. And it is no disgrace these days to pose as an artist's model. The classic oils, nowadays, call only for exquisite creations in gowns and hats; mythology was exhausted by the old masters. Rome, Paris, London; possibly a bohemian existence in these cities accounted for her ease in striking up a conversation, harmless enough, with a total stranger. In Paris and Rome it was all very well; but it is a risky thing to do in unromantic New York and London. However, her uncle had been with her; a veritable fortress, had I over-stepped the bounds of politeness.

The smoke wavered and rolled about me. I took out the ten of hearts and studied it musingly. After all, should I go? Would it be wise? I confess I saw goblins' heads peering from the spots, and old Poe stories returned to me! Pshaw! It was only a frolic, no serious harm could possibly come of it. I would certainly go, now I had gone thus far. What fool idea the girl was bent on I hadn't the least idea; but I easily recognized the folly upon which I was about to set sail. Heigh-ho! What was a lonely young bachelor to do? At the most, they could only ask me to vacate the premises, should I be so unfortunate as to be discovered. In that event, Teddy Hamilton would come to my assistance. . . . She was really beautiful! And then I awoke to the alarming fact that the girl in Mouquin's was interesting me more than I liked to confess.

Presently, through the haze of smoke, I saw a patch of white paper on the rug in front of the pier-glass. I rose and picked it up.

NAME: *Hawthorne*   COSTUME: *Blue Domino*   TIME: *5:30 P. M.*   RETURNED: ADDRESS: *West 87th Street*
        FRIARD'S

I stared at the bit of pasteboard, fascinated. How the deuce had this got into my apartments? A Blue Domino? Ha! I had it! Old Friard had accidentally done up the ticket with my mask. A

Blue Domino; evidently I wasn't the only person who was going to a masquerade. Without doubt this fair demoiselle was about to join the festivities of some shop-girls' masquerade, where money and pedigree are inconsequent things, and where everybody is either a "loidy" or a "gent." Persons who went to my kind of masquerade did not rent their costumes; they laid out extravagant sums to the fashionable modiste and tailor, and had them made to order. A Blue Domino: humph!

It was too late to take the ticket back to Friard's; so I determined to mail it to him in the morning.

It was now high time for me to be off. I got into my coat and took down my opera hat. Outside the storm was still active; but the snow had a promising softness, and there were patches of stars to be seen here and there in the sky. By midnight there would be a full moon. I got to Jersey City without mishap; and when I took my seat in the smoker, I found I had ten minutes to spare. I bought a newspaper and settled down to read the day's news. It was fully half an hour between Jersey City and Blankshire; in that time I could begin and finish the paper.

There never was a newspaper those days that hadn't a war-map in some one of its columns; and when I had digested the latest phases of the war in the far East, I quite naturally turned to the sporting-page to learn what was going on among the other professional fighters. (Have I mentioned to you the fact that I was all through the Spanish War, the mix-up in China, and that I had resigned my commission to accept the post of traveling salesman for a famous motor-car company? If I have not, pardon me. You will now readily accept my recklessness of spirit as a matter of course.) I turned over another page; from this I learned that the fair sex was going back to puff-sleeves again. Many an old sleeve was going to be turned upside down.

Fudge! The train was rattling through the yards. Another page crackled. Ha! Here was that unknown gentleman-thief again, up to his old tricks. It is remarkable how difficult it is to catch a thief who has good looks and shrewd brains. I had already written him down as a quasi-swell. For months the police had been finding clues, but they had never laid eyes on the rascal. The famous Haggerty of the New York detective force,— a man whom not a dozen New York policemen knew by sight and no criminals save those behind bars, earthly and eternal,—was now giving his whole attention to the affair. Some gaily-dressed lady at a ball would suddenly find she had lost some valuable gems; and that would be the end of the affair, for none ever recovered her gems.

The gentleman-thief was still at large, and had gathered to his account a comfortable fortune; that is, if he were not already rich and simply a kleptomaniac. No doubt he owned one of my racing-cars, and was clear of the delinquent lists at his clubs. I dismissed all thought of him, threw aside the paper, and mentally figured out my commissions on sales during the past month. It was a handsome figure, large enough for two. This pastime, too, soon failed to interest me. I gazed out of the window and watched the dark shapes as they sped past.

I saw the girl's face from time to time. What a fool I had been not to ask her name! She could easily have refused, and yet as easily have granted the request. At any rate, I had permitted the chance to slip out of my reach, which was exceedingly careless on my part. Perhaps they—she and her uncle—frequently dined at Mouquin's; I determined to haunt the place and learn. It would be easy enough to address her the next time we met. Besides, she would be curious to know all about the ten of hearts and the desperate adventure upon which I told her I was about to embark. Many a fine friendship has grown out of smaller things.

Next, turning from the window, I fell to examining my fellow passengers, in the hope of seeing some one I knew. Conversation on trains makes short journeys. . . . I sat up stiffly in my seat. Diagonally across the aisle sat the very chap I had met in the curio-shop! He was quietly reading a popular magazine, and occasionally a smile lightened his sardonic mouth. Funny that I should run across him twice in the same evening! Men who are contemplating suicide never smile in that fashion. He was smoking a small, well-colored meerschaum pipe with evident relish. Somehow, when a man clenches his teeth upon the mouth-piece of a respectable pipe, it seems impossible to associate that man with crime. But the fact that I had seen him selecting a pistol in a pawnshop rather neutralized the good opinion I was willing to form. I have already expressed my views upon the subject. The sight of him rather worried me, though I could not reason why. Whither was he bound? Had he finally taken one of Friard's pistols? For a moment I was on the point of speaking to him, if only to hear him tell more lies about the ten of hearts, but I wisely put aside the temptation. Besides, it might be possible that he would not be glad to see me. I always avoid the chance acquaintance, unless, of course, the said chance acquaintance is met under favorable circumstances—like the girl in Mouquin's, for instance! After all, it was only an incident; and, but for his picking up that card, I never should have remembered him.

Behind him sat a fellow with a countenance as red and round and complacent as an English butler's,—red hair and small twinkling eyes. Once he leaned over and spoke to my chance acquaintance, who, without turning his head, thrust a match over his shoulder. The man with the face of a butler lighted the most villainous pipe I ever beheld. I wondered if they knew each other. But, closely as I watched, I saw no sign from either. I turned my collar up and snuggled down. There was no need of his seeing *me*.

Then my thoughts reverted to the ten of hearts again. My ten of hearts! The wrinkle of a chill ran up and down my spine! My ten of hearts!

Hastily I took out the card and examined the *back* of it. It was an uncommonly handsome back, representing Diana, the moon, and the midnight sky. A horrible supposition came to me: supposing they looked at the back as well as at the face of the card? And again, supposing I was miles away from the requisite color and design? I was staggered. Here was a pretty fix! I had never even dreamed of such a contingency. Hang it! I now wished I had stuck to my original plan, and gone to the theater. Decidedly I was in for it; there was no backing down at this late hour, unless I took the return train for Jersey City; and I possessed too much stubbornness to surrender to any such weakness. Either I should pass the door-committee, or I shouldn't; of one thing I was certain—

"Blankshire!" bawled the trainman; then the train slowed down and finally came to a stop.

No turning back for me now. I picked up my suit-case and got out. On the platform I saw the curio-shop fellow again. Tramping on ahead, the smell from his villainous pipe assailing my nostrils, was the man who had asked for a match. The former stood undecided for a moment, and during this space of time he caught sight of me. He became erect, gave me a sudden sardonic laugh, and swiftly disappeared into the dark. All this was uncommonly disquieting; in vain I stared into the blackness that had swallowed him. What could he be doing here at Blankshire? I didn't like his laugh at all; there was at once a menace and a challenge in it.

"Any baggage, sir?" asked one of the station hands.

"No." But I asked him to direct me to a hotel. He did so.

I made my way down the street. The wind had veered around and was coming in from the sea, pure and cold. The storm-clouds were broken and scudding like dark ships, and at times there were flashes of radiant moonshine.

The fashionable hotel was full. So I plodded through the drifts to the unfashionable hotel. Here I found accommodation. I dressed, sometimes laughing, sometimes whistling, sometimes standing motionless in doubt. Bah! It was only a lark. . . . I thought of the girl in Mouquin's; how much better it would have been to spend the evening with her, exchanging badinage, and looking into each other's eyes! Pshaw! I covered my face with the grey mask and descended to the street.

The trolley ran within two miles of the Hunt Club. The car was crowded with masqueraders, and for the first time since I started out I felt comfortable. Everybody laughed and talked, though nobody knew who his neighbor was. I sat in a corner, silent and motionless as a sphinx. Once a pair of blue slippers attracted my eye, and again the flash of a lovely arm. At the end of the trolley line was a carryall which was to convey us to the club. We got into the conveyance, noisily and good-humoredly. The exclamations of the women were amusing.

"Good gracious!"

"Isn't it fun!"

"Lovely!" And all that. It must have been a novelty for some of these to act naturally for once. Nothing lasts so long as the natural instinct for play; and we always find ourselves coming back to it.

Standing some hundred yards back from the road was the famous Hollywood Inn, run by the genial Moriarty. Sometimes the members of the Hunt Club put up there for the night when there was to be a run the following morning. It was open all the year round.

We made the club at exactly ten-thirty. Fortune went with me; doubtless it was the crowd going in that saved me from close scrutiny. My spirits rose as I espied Teddy Hamilton at the door. He was on the committee, and was in plain evening clothes. It was good to see a familiar face. I shouldered toward him and passed out my ten dollars.

"Hello, Teddy, my son!" I cried out jovially.

"Hello!"—grinning. Teddy thought it was some one he knew; well, so it was. "What's your card?" he cried, as I pressed by him.

"The ten of hearts."

"The ten of hearts," repeated Teddy to a man who was keeping tally on a big cardboard.

This sight did not reassure me. If they were keeping tally of all the cards presented at the door, they would soon find out that there were too many tens of hearts, too many by one! Well, at any rate, I had for the time being escaped detection; now for the fun. It would be sport-royal while it lasted. What a tale to give out at the club of a Sunday night! I chuckled on the way to the ball-room: I had dispensed with going up to the dressing-room. My robe was a genuine one, heavy and warm; so I had no overcoat to check.

"Grave monk, your blessing!"

Turning, I beheld an exquisite Columbine.

"*Pax vobiscum!*" I replied solemnly.

"*Pax* . . . What does that mean?"

"It means, do not believe all you see in the

newspapers."

Columbine laughed gaily. "I did not know that you were a Latin scholar; and besides, you gave me to understand you were coming as a Jesuit, Billy."

Billy? Here was one who thought she knew me. I hastened to disillusion her.

"My dear Columbine, you do not know me, not the least bit. My name is not Billy, it is Dicky."

"Oh, you can not fool me," she returned. "I heard you call out to Teddy Hamilton that your card was the ten of hearts; and you wrote me, saying that would be your card."

Complications already, and I hadn't yet put a foot inside the ball-room!

"I am sorry," I said, "but you have made a mistake. Your Jesuit probably told you his card would be the nine, not the ten."

"I will wager—"

"Hush! This is a charity dance; no one makes wagers at such affairs."

"But—Why, my goodness! there's my Jesuit now!" And to my intense relief she dashed away.

I carefully observed the Jesuit, and made up my mind to keep an eye upon him. If he really possessed the ten of hearts, the man who kept tally on the cardboard was doing some tall thinking about this time. I glided away, into the gorgeous ball-room.

What a vision greeted my eye! The decorations were in red and yellow, and it seemed as though perpetual autumnal sunset lay over everything. At the far end of the room was a small stage hidden behind palms and giant ferns. The band was just striking up *A Summer Night in Munich*, and a wonderful kaleidoscope revolved around me. I saw Cavaliers and Roundheads, Puritans and Beelzebubs, Musketeers, fools, cowboys, Indians, kings and princes; queens and empresses, fairies and Quaker maids, white and black and red and green dominoes. Tom Fool's night, indeed!

Presently I saw the noble Doge of Venice coming my way. From his portly carriage I reasoned that if he wasn't in the gold-book of Venice he stood very well up in the gold-book of New York, He stopped at my side and struck an attitude.

"*Pax vobiscum!*" said I, bowing.

"Be at the Inquisition Chamber, directly the clock strikes the midnight hour," he said mysteriously.

"I shall be there to deliver the supreme interrogation," I replied.

"It is well." He drifted away like a stately ship.

Delightful foolery! I saw the Jesuit, and moved toward him.

"Disciple of Loyola, hast thou the ten of hearts?"

"My hearts number nine, for I have lost one to the gay Columbine."

"I breathe! Thou art not he whom I seek."

We separated. I was mortally glad that Columbine had made a mistake.

The women always seek the monk at a masquerade; they want absolution for the follies they are about to commit. A demure Quakeress touched my sleeve in passing.

"Tell me, grave monk, why did you seek the monastery?"

"My wife fell in love with me,"—gloomily.

"Then you have a skeleton in the clothes-press?"

"Do I look like a man who owned such a thing as a clothes-press, much less so fashionable a thing as a family skeleton?"

"Then what do you here?"

"I am mingling with fools as a penance."

A fool caught me by the sleeve and batted me gaily over the head with a bladder.

"Merry come up, why am I a fool?"

"It is the fashion," was my answer. This was like to gain me the reputation of being a wit. I must walk carefully, or these thoughtless ones would begin to suspect there was an impostor among them.

"Aha!" There was mine ancient friend Julius. "Hail Caesar!"

He stopped.

"Shall I beware the Ides of March?" I asked jovially.

"Nay, my good Cassius; rather beware of the ten of hearts," said Caesar in hollow tones, and he was gone.

The ten of hearts again! Hang the card! And then with a sigh of relief I recollected that in all probability he, like Columbine, had heard me call out the card to Hamilton. Still, the popularity of the card was very disquieting. I wished it had been seven or five; there's luck in odd numbers. . . . A Blue Domino! My heart leaped, and I thought of the little ticket in my waistcoat pocket. A Blue Domino! If, by chance, there should be a connection between her and the ticket!

She was sitting all alone in a corner near-by, partly screened by a pot of orange-trees. I crossed over and sat down by her side. This might prove an adventure worth while.

"What a beautiful night it is!" I said.

She turned, and I caught sight of a wisp of golden hair.

"That is very original," said she. "Who in the world would have thought of passing comments on the weather at a masque! Prior to this moment the men have been calling me all sorts of sentimental names."

"Oh, I am coming to that. I am even going to make love to you."

She folded her hands,—rather resignedly, I thought,—and the rollicking comedy began.

III

When they give you a mask at a ball they also give you the key to all manner of folly and impudence. Even stupid persons become witty, and the witty become correspondingly daring. For all I knew, the Blue Domino at my side might be Jones' wife, or Brown's, or Smith's, or even Green's; but so long as I was not certain, it mattered not in what direction my whimsical fancy took me. (It is true that ordinarily Jones and Brown and Smith and Green do not receive invitations to attend masquerades at fashionable hunt clubs; but somehow they seem to worry along without these equivocal honors, and prosper. Still, there are persons in the swim named Johnes and Smythe and Browne and Greene. Pardon this parenthesis!)

As I recollected the manner in which I had self-invited the pleasure of my company to this carnival at the Blankshire Hunt Club, I smiled behind my mask. Nerves! I ought to have been a professor of clinics instead of an automobile agent. But the whole affair appealed to me so strongly I could not resist it. I was drawn into the tangle by the very fascination of the scheme. I was an interloper, but nobody knew it. The ten of hearts in my pocket did not match the backs of those cards regularly issued. But what of that? Every one was ignorant of the fact. I was safe inside; and all that was romantic in my system was aroused. There are always some guests who can not avail themselves of their invitations; and upon this vague chance I had staked my play. Besides, I was determined to disappear before the hour of unmasking. I wasn't going to take any unnecessary risks. I was, then, fairly secure under my Capuchin's robe.

Out of my mind slipped the previous adventures of the evening. I forgot, temporarily, the beautiful unknown at Mouquin's. I forgot the sardonic-lipped stranger I had met in Friard's. I forgot everything save the little ticket that had accidentally slipped into my package, and which announced that some one had rented a blue domino.

And here was a Blue Domino at my side. Just simply dying to have me talk to her!

"I am madly in love with you," I began. "I have followed you often; I have seen you in your box at the opera; I have seen you whirl up Fifth Avenue in your fine barouche; and here at last I meet you!" I clasped my hands passionately.

"My beautiful barouche! My box at the opera!" the girl mimicked. "What a cheerful Ananias you are!"

"Thou art the most enchanting creature in all the universe. Thou art even as a turquoise, a patch of radiant summer sky, eyes of sapphire, lips—"

"Archaic, very archaic," she interrupted.

"Disillusioned in ten seconds!" I cried dismally. "How could you?"

She laughed.

"Have you no romance? Can you not see the fitness of things? If you have not a box at the opera, you ought at least to make believe you have. History walks about us, and you call the old style archaic! That hurts!"

"Methinks, Sir Monk—"

"There! That's more like it. By my halidom, that's the style!"

"Odds bodkins, you don't tell me!" There was a second ripple of laughter from behind the mask. It was rare music.

"I *could* fall in love with you!"

"There once was a Frenchman who said that as nothing is impossible, let us believe in the absurd. I might be old enough to be your grandmother,"—lightly.

"Perish the thought!"

"Perish it, indeed!"

"The mask is the thing!" I cried enthusiastically. "You can make love to another man's wife—"

"Or to your own, and nobody is the wiser,"—cynically.

"We are getting on."

"Yes, we are getting on, both in years and in folly. What are you doing in a monk's robe? Where is your motley, gay fool?"

"I have laid it aside for the night. On such occasions as this, fools dress as wise men, and wise men as fools; everybody goes about in disguise."

"How would you go about to pick out the fools?"—curiously.

"Beginning with myself—"

"Thy name is also Candor!"

"Look at yonder Cavalier. He wabbles like a ship in distress, in the wild effort to keep his feet untangled from his rapier. I'll wager he's a wealthy plumber on week-days. Observe Anne of

Austria! What arms! I'll lay odds that her great-grandmother took in washing. There's Romeo, now, with a pair of legs like an old apple tree. The freedom of criticism is mine to-night! Did you ever see such ridiculous ideas of costume? For my part, the robe and the domino for me. All lines are destroyed; nothing is recognizable. My, my! There's Harlequin, too, walking on parentheses."

The Blue Domino laughed again.

"You talk as if you had no friends here,"—shrewdly.

"But which is my friend and which is the man to whom I owe money?"

"What! Is your tailor here then?"

"Heaven forbid! Strange, isn't it, when a fellow starts in to pay up his bills, that the tailor and the undertaker have to wait till the last."

"The subject is outside my understanding."

"But you have dressmakers."

"I seldom pay dressmakers."

"Ah! Then you belong to the most exclusive set!"

"Or perhaps I make my own dresses—"

"Sh! Not so loud. Supposing some one should overhear you?"

"It was a slip of the tongue. And yet, you should be lenient to all."

"Kind heart! Ah, I wonder what all those interrogation points mean—the black domino there?"

"Possibly she represents Scandal."

"Scandal, then, is symbolized by the interrogation point?"

"Yes. Whoever heard of scandal coming to a full stop, that is to say, a period."

"I learn something every minute. A hundred years ago you would have been a cousin to Mademoiselle de Necker."

"Or Madame de Stael."

"Oh, if you are married—"

"I shall have ceased to interest you?"

"On the contrary. Only, marriage would account for the bitterness of your tone. What does the Blue Domino represent?"

"The needle of the compass." She stretched a sleeve out toward me and I observed for the first time the miniature compasses woven in the cloth. Surely, one does not rent a costume like this.

"I understand now why you attracted me. Whither will you guide me?'"—sentimentally.

"Through dark channels and stormy seas, over tropic waters, 'into the haven under the hill.'"

"Oh, if you go to quoting Tennyson, it's all up with me. *Are* you married?"

"One can easily see that at any rate *you* are not."

"Explain."

"Your voice lacks the proper and requisite anxiety. It is always the married woman who enjoys the mask with thoroughness. She knows her husband will be watching her; and jealousy is a good sign."

"You are a philosopher. Certainly you must be married."

"Well, one does become philosophical—after marriage."

"But are you married?"

"I do not say so."

"Would you like to be?"

"I have my share of feminine curiosity. But I wonder,"— ruminating, "why they do not give masquerades oftener."

"That is easily explained. Most of us live masquerades day by day, and there might be too much of a good thing."

"That is a bit of philosophy that goes well with your robe. Indeed, what better mask is there than the human countenance?"

"If we become serious, we shall put folly out of joint," said I, rising. "And besides, we shall miss the best part of this dance."

She did not hesitate an instant. I led her to the floor, and we joined the dancers. She was as light as a feather, a leaf, the down of the thistle; mysterious as the Cumaean Sibyl; and I wondered who she might be. The hand that lay on my sleeve was as white as milk, and the filbert-shaped horn of the finger-tips was the tint of rose leaves. *Was* she connected with the ticket in my pocket? I tried to look into her eyes, but in vain; nothing could I see but that wisp of golden hair which occasionally brushed my chin as with a surreptitious caress. If only I dared remain till the unmasking! I pressed her hand. There was an answering pressure, but its tenderness was destroyed by the low laughter that accompanied it.

"Don't be silly!" she whispered.

"How can I help it?"

"True; I forgot you were a fool in disguise."

"What has Romance done to you that you should turn on her with the stuffed-club, Practicality?"

"She has never paid any particular attention to me; perhaps that is the reason."

As we neared a corner I saw the Honorable Julius again. He stretched forth his death's-head mask.

"Beware the ten of hearts!" he croaked.

Hang his impudence! . . . The Blue Domino turned her head with a jerk; and instantly I felt a shiver run through her body. For a moment she lost step. I was filled with wonder. In what manner could the ten of hearts disturb *her*? I made up my mind to seek out the noble Roman and learn just how much he knew about that disquieting card.

The music ceased.

"Now, run away with your benedictions," said the Blue Domino breathlessly.

"Shall I see you again?"—eagerly.

"If you seek diligently." She paused for a moment, like a bird about to take flight. "Positive, fool; comparative, fooler; superlative, foolest!"

And I was left standing alone: What the deuce did she mean by that?

After all, there might be any number of blue dominoes in the land; and it seemed scarcely credible that a guest at the Hunt Club would go to a costumer's for an outfit. (I had gone to a costumer's, but my case was altogether different. I was an impostor.) I hunted up *Imperator Rex.* It was not long ere we came face to face, or, to speak correctly, mask to mask.

"What do you know about the ten of hearts?" I began with directness.

"I am a shade; all things are known to me."

"You may be a lamp-shade, for all I care. What do you know about the ten of hearts?"

"Beware of it,"—hollowly. From under his toga he produced a ten of hearts!

My knees wabbled, and there was a sense of looseness about my collar. The fellow *knew* I was an impostor. Why didn't he denounce me?

"Is the back of your card anything like this one?"—ironically.
"I dare say it isn't. But have your good time, grave monk;
doubtless you are willing that the fiddlers shall be paid." And
wrapping his toga about him majestically, he stalked away,
leaving me staring dumfoundedly after his receding form.

Discovered!

The deuce! Had I been attired like yon Romeo, I certainly
should have taken to my heels; but a fellow can not run in a
Capuchin's gown, and retain any dignity. I would much rather
be arrested than laughed at. I stood irresolute. What was to be
done? How much did he know? Did he know who I was? And
what was his object in letting me run my course? I was all at
sea. . . . Hang the grisly old Roman! I shut my teeth; I would
see the comedy to its end, no matter what befell. If worst came
to worst, there was always Teddy Hamilton to fall back on.

I made off toward the smoking-room, rumbling imprecations
against the gods for having given me the idea of attending this
masquerade, when it would have been cheaper and far more
comfortable to go to the theater.

But as soon as I entered the smoking-room, I laughed. It was
a droll scene. Here we were, all of us, trying savagely to smoke a
cigar or cigarette through the flabby aperture designated in a
mask as the mouth. It was a hopeless job; for myself, I gave it
up in disgust.

Nobody dared talk naturally for fear of being identified.
When a man did open his mouth it was only to commit some
banal idiocy, for which, during office hours, he would have been
haled to the nearest insane asylum and labeled incurable.
Added to this was a heat matching Sahara's and the oppressive
odor of weltering paint.

By Jove! Only one man knew that the back of my card was
unlike the others: the man who had picked it up in old Friard's
curio-shop, the man who had come to Blankshire with me! I
knew now. He had been there buying a costume like myself. He
had seen me on the train, and had guessed the secret. I elbowed
my way out of the smoking-room. It wouldn't do me a bit of
harm to ask a few polite questions of Mr. Caesar of the sardonic
laugh.

But I had lost the golden opportunity. Caesar had gone to
join the shades of other noble Romans; in vain I searched high

and low for him. Once I ran into Hamilton. His face was pale and disturbed and anxious.

"What's the trouble, Hamilton?" I asked, with forced gaiety.

He favored me with a penetrating glance.

"The very devil is the trouble," he growled. "Several of the ladies have begun to miss valuable jewels. Anne of Austria has lost her necklace and Queen Elizabeth is without a priceless comb; altogether, about ten thousand dollars."

"Robbery?" I looked at him aghast.

"That's the word. Curse the luck! There is always something of this sort happening to spoil the fun. But whoever has the jewels will not get away with them."

"What are you going to do?"

"I have already sent for the village police. Now I shall lock all the doors and make every man and woman produce cards for identification,"—abruptly leaving me.

Thunderbolts out of heaven! My knees and collar bothered me again; the first attack was trifling compared to this second seizure. How the devil was I to get out?

"Are you searching for me?" inquired a soft voice at my elbow.

I turned instantly. The Blue Domino had come back to me.

"I have been searching for you everywhere," I said gallantly.

"Oh! but that is a black one. Never mind; the fib was well meant."

I led her over to a secluded nook, within a few feet of the door which gave entrance to the club cellars. This door I had been bearing in mind for some time. It is well to know your topography. The door was at the left of the band platform. There was a twin-door on the other side. We sat down.

"Have you heard the news?" I asked.

"No. Has some one been discovered making love to his own wife by mistake?"

"It's serious. Anne of Austria and Queen Elizabeth have been robbed of some jewels."

"A thief among us?"

"A regular Galloping Dick. I'm a thief myself, for that matter."

"You?" she drew away from me a bit.

"Yes. My name is Procrastination."

"Ah, my grave Capuchin, we do not steal time; we merely waste it. But is what you tell me true?"

"I am very sorry to say it is. The jewels were worth something like ten thousand dollars."

"Merciful heavens!"

"It is true, infernally true,"—looking around to see if by chance Caesar had reappeared on the scene. (How was I to manage my escape? It is true I might hie me to the cellars; but how to get out of the cellars!) "Have you seen Julius Caesar?" I asked.

"Caesar?"

"Yes, Miss Hawthorne—"

The Blue Domino swung about and leaned toward me, her hands tense upon the sides of her chair.

"What name did you say?"—a strained note in her voice.

"Hawthorne," I answered, taking out the slip of pasteboard. "See! it says that one blue domino was rented of Monsieur Friard at five-thirty this afternoon."

"How did you come by that ticket?" she demanded.

"It was a miracle. I purchased a mask there, and this ticket was wrapped up in my bundle by mistake."

"It is a curious coincidence,"—her voice normal and unagitated.

I was confused. "Then I am mistaken?"—my chagrin evident. (All this while, mind you, I was wondering if that cellar-door was unlocked, and how long it would take me to reach it before the denouement!)

"One way or the other, it does not matter," said she.

"Yet, if I could reach the cellars,"—absently. Then I bit my tongue.

"Cellars? Who said anything about cellars? I meant that this is not the hour for unmasking or disclosing one's identity,"—coldly.

"And yet, when Caesar whispered 'Beware the ten of hearts' you turned and shuddered. What have you to offer in defense?"

"It was the horrid mask he wore."

"Well, it wasn't handsome of him."

"What did you mean by cellars?"—suddenly becoming the inquisitor in her turn.

"I? Oh, I was thinking what I should do in case of fire,"—nimbly.

"That is not the truth."

"Well, no, it isn't. Can you keep a secret?" I whispered.

"If it isn't a terrible one."

"Well, I have no earthly business here. I am an impostor."

"An impostor!"

"Yes. And for the past few minutes, since I heard of the robbery, I've been thinking how I could get out of here upon the slightest notice." While the reckless spirit was upon me, I produced the fatal card and showed the back to her. "You will find that yours is of a different color. But *I* am not the Galloping Dick; it was only a hare-brained lark on my part, and I had no idea it would turn out serious like this. I was going to disappear before they unmasked. What would you advise me to do?"

She took the card, studied it, and finally returned it. There followed an interval of silence.

"I have known the imposition from the first," she said.

"What!"

She touched the signet-ring on my little finger. "I have seen that once before to-night. No," she mused, "you will not blow up the post-office to-night, nor the police-station."

She lifted the corner of her mask, and I beheld the girl I had met in Mouquin's!

"You?"

"Silence! So this is the meaning of your shuffling those cards? Oh, it is certainly droll!" She laughed.

"And are you Miss Hawthorne?"

"I am still in the mask, sir; I shall answer none of your questions."

"This is the finest romance in the world!" I cried.

"You were talking about getting out," she said. "Shall I lend you my domino? But that would be useless. Such a prestidigitator as Signor Fantoccini has only to say—Presto! and disappear at once."

"I assure you, it is no laughing matter."

"I see it from a different angle."

An artist's model, and yet a guest at this exclusive function?

A commotion around the stage distracted us. Presently we saw Teddy Hamilton mount the stage and hold up his hands.

"Attention, ladies and gentlemen!" he called.

Silence gradually fell upon the motley groups of masqueraders.

"A thief is among us. I have had all the exits closed. Everybody will be so kind as to present cards at the main entrance. Three ten-spots of hearts have been tallied on the comparing lists. We have been imposed upon. The police are on the way. Very sorry to cause you this annoyance. The identity of the holders of the cards will be known only to those of us on the committee."

Silence and then a murmur which soon became a fuzzing like that of many bees.

The Blue Domino suddenly clutched my arm.

"Please take me away, take me away at once! I'm an impostor, too!"

Two of us!

This was disaster. I give you my solemn word, there was nothing I regretted so much as the fact that I hadn't gone to the theater.

But I am a man of quick thought and resource. In the inelegant phrasing of the day, me for the cellars!

"Come," said I to the girl; "There's only one chance in a hundred, but we'll take it together."

"Together? Where?"

"Why, to the cellars. I've a pocketful of matches. We can make a try. For, if there's a thief around, and we are caught and proved impostors—Well, I leave you to imagine!"

"I will go with you," she replied resolutely.

The gods were with us. The door leading to the cellars was not locked. I opened it, passed the girl before me, and closed the door.

"I am frightened!" she whispered.

"So am I," I offered, to reassure her. "You are not afraid of rats, are you?"

"No-o!"

"Bully!" I cried. Then I laughed.

"How *can* you laugh? It is horrible!" she protested.

"You would come, though I heard your uncle warn you. Look at it the way I do. It's a huge joke, and years from now you'll have great fun telling it to your grandchildren."

"I wish, at this moment, I could see so far ahead—What was that?"—seizing my arm.

Click!

Somebody had locked the door behind us!

IV

In other words, we had departed the scene of festivities none too soon. I could readily understand why the door had been locked: it was not to keep us in the cellars; rather it was to prevent any one from leaving the ball-room by that route. Evidently our absence had not been noticed, nor had any seen our precipitate flight. I sighed gratefully.

For several minutes we stood silent and motionless on the landing. At length I boldly struck a match. The first thing that greeted my blinded gaze was the welcome vision of a little shelf lined with steward's candles. One of these I lighted, and two others I stuffed into the pocket of my Capuchin's gown. Then we tiptoed softly down the stairs, the girl tugging fearfully at my sleeve.

There was an earthy smell. It was damp and cold. Miles and miles away (so it seemed) the pale moonshine filtered through a cobwebbed window, It was ghostly; but so far as I was concerned, I was honestly enjoying myself, strange as this statement may seem. Here was I, setting forth upon an adventure with the handsomest, wittiest girl I had ever laid eyes upon. If I extricated her neatly, she would always be in my debt; and the thought of this was mighty pleasant to contemplate.

"Do you know the way out?"

I confessed that, so far as I knew, we were in one of the fabled labyrinths of mythology.

"Go ahead," she said bravely.

"I ask only to die in your Highness' service,"—soberly.

"But I do not want you to die; I want you to get me out of this cellar; and quickly, too."

"I'll live or die in the attempt!"

"I see nothing funny in our predicament,"—icily.

"A few moments ago you said that our angles of vision were not the same; I begin to believe it. As for me, I think it's simply immense to find myself in the same boat with you."

"I wish you *had* been an anarchist, or a performer in a dime-museum."

"You might now be alone here. But, pardon me; surely you do not lack the full allotment of the adventurous spirit! It was all amusing enough to come here under false pretenses."

"But I had not reckoned on any one's losing jewels."

"No more had I."

"Proceed. I have the courage to trust to your guidance."

"I would that it might be always!"—with a burst of sentiment that was not wholly feigned.

"Let us be on,"—imperatively. "I shall not only catch my death of cold, but I shall be horribly compromised."

"My dear young lady, on the word of a gentleman, I will do the best I can to get you out of this cellar. If I have jested a little, it was only in the effort to give you courage; for I haven't the slightest idea how we are going to get out of this dismal hole."

We went on. We couldn't see half a dozen feet in front of us. The gloom beyond the dozen feet was Stygian and menacing. And the great grim shadows that crept behind us as we proceeded! Once the girl stumbled and fell against me.

"What's the matter?" I asked, startled.

"I stepped on something that—that moved!"—plaintively.

"Possibly it was a potato; there's a bin of them over there. Where the deuce are we?"

"If you swear, I shall certainly scream!" she warned.

"But I can swear in the most elegant and approved fashion."

"I am not inclined to have you demonstrate your talents."

"Aha! Here is the coal-bin. Perhaps the window may be open. If so, we are saved. Will you hold the candle for a moment?"

Have you ever witnessed a cat footing it across the snow? If you have, picture me imitating her. Cautiously I took one step, then another; and then that mountain of coal turned into a roaring tread-mill. Sssssh! Rrrrr! In a moment I was buried to the knees and nearly suffocated. I became angry. I would reach that window—

"Hush! Hush! The noise, the noise!" whispered the girl, waving the candle frantically.

But I was determined. Again I tried. This time I slipped and fell on my hands. As I strove to get up, the cord of my gown became tangled about my feet. The girl choked; whether with coal-dust or with laughter I could not say, as she still had on her cambric-mask.

"Forgive me," she said. And then I knew it was not the coal-dust.

"I'll forgive you, but I will not promise to forget."

"Merciful heavens! you must not try that again. Think of the noise!"

"Was I making any noise?"—rubbing the perspiration from my forehead. (I had taken off my mask.)

"Noise? The trump of Judgment Day will be feeble compared to it. Surely some one has heard you. Why not lay that board on top of the coal?"

A good idea. I made use of it at once. The window was unlatched, but there was a heavy wire-screen nailed to the sills outside. There was no getting out that way. The gods were evidently busy elsewhere.

"Nothing doing," I murmured, a bit discouraged.

"And even if there was, you really could not expect me to risk my neck and dignity by climbing through a window like that. Let us give up the idea of windows and seek the cellar-doors, those that give to the grounds. I declare I shall leave by no other exit."

"It was very kind of you to let me make an ass of myself like that. Why didn't you tell me beforehand?"

"Perhaps it's the angle of vision again. I can see that we shall never agree. Seriously, I thought that if you got out that way, you might find the other exit for me. I am sorry if my laughter annoyed you."

"Not at all, not at all. But wouldn't it be wise to save a little laughter to make merry with when we get out?"

I stepped out of the bin and relieved her of the candle; and we went on.

"You did look funny," she said.

"Please don't!" I begged.

Soon we came to a bin of cabbages. I peered in philosophically.

"I might find a better head in there than mine," I suggested.

"Now you are trying to be sarcastic," said the girl.

We went on.

"Wait a moment!" she cried. "Here's a bin of nice apples."

Apples! Well, my word, she was a cool one! I picked up one, polished it on my sleeve, and gave it to her.

"I'm hungry," she said apologetically.

"And plucky, too," I supplemented admiringly. "Most women would be in a weeping state by this time."

"Perhaps I am waiting till it is all over."

"You had better take off your mask." In fact I felt positive that the sight of her exquisite face would act like a tonic upon my nerves.

"I am doing very well with it on. I can at least keep my face clean." She raised the curtain and took a liberal bite of the apple—so nonchalantly that I was forced to smile.

"Here's a box," said I; "let's sit down while we eat. We are safe enough. If any one had heard the racket in the coal-bin, the cellar would have been full of police by this time."

And there we sat, calmly munching the apples, for all the world as if the iron hand of the law wasn't within a thousand miles of us. It was all very amusing.

"Are—*are* you the man they are hunting for?" she asked abruptly.

"I never stole anything more terrible than green apples—and ripe ones"—with a nod toward the apple-bin.

"Pardon me! I feel very guilty in asking you such a question. You haven't told me your name."

"Haven't I? My name is Richard Comstalk. My friends call me Dickey."

"Dickey," she murmured. "It's a nice name."

"Won't you have another apple?" I asked impulsively.

"My appetite is appeased, thank you."

An idea came to me. "Hamilton said there were three tens of hearts. That meant that only one was out of order. Where did you get your card?"

"That I shall tell you—later."

"But are you really an impostor?"

"I should not be in this cellar else."

"You are very mystifying."

"For the present I prefer to remain so."

We tossed aside the apple-cores, rose, and went on. It was the longest cellar *I* ever saw. There seemed absolutely no end to it. The wine-cellar was walled apart from the main cellar, and had the semblance of a huge cistern with a door opening into it. As we passed it, the vague perfume of the grape drifted out to us.

"Let's have a bottle," I began.

"Mr. Comstalk!"

"By absent-treatment!" I hastened to add.

"You will make a capital comrade—if we ever get out of this cellar."

"Trust me for that!" I replied gaily. "Be careful; there's a pile of empty bottles, yearning to be filled with tomato-catsup. Give me your hand."

But the moment the little digits closed over mine, a thrill seized me, and I quickly bent my head and kissed the hand. It was wrong, but I could not help it. She neither spoke nor withdrew her hand; and my fear that she might really be offended vanished.

"We are nearly out of it," I said exultantly. "I see the cellar-stairs on ahead. If only those doors are open!"

"Heaven is merciful to the fool, and we are a pair," she replied, sighing gratefully. "It seems strange that nobody should be in the cellar on a night like this. Hark! They are playing again up stairs in the ball-room."

"And wondering a whole lot where that third ten of hearts has gone."

"But, listen. How are we to get back to the trolley? We certainly can not walk the distance in these clothes."

"Oh, that carryall will come to our rescue. We are weary and are leaving early, don't you know? That part is simple; the complicated thing is to shake the dust of this cellar."

"What a big furnace!" she exclaimed, as we came into view of the huge heating apparatus. "And there's more coal."

A man stepped out from behind the furnace, and confronted us. A red bandana covered the lower part of his face and his hat was pulled down over his eyes. But I recognized him instantly. It was the fellow with the villainous pipe! Something glittered ominously at the end of his outstretched arm.

"If you make any noise, sir, I'll have to plug you, sir," he said in polite but muffled tones.

The candle slipped from my fingers, and the three of us stood in darkness!

V

There was a clicking sound, and the glare of a dark-lantern struck my blinking eyes.

"Pick up the candle, sir," said the tranquil voice from behind the light.

I obeyed readily enough. Fate was downright cruel to us. Not a dozen feet away was liberty; and now we were back at the beginning again, with the end nowhere in sight.

"Shall I light it, sir?" I asked, not to be outdone in the matter of formal politeness.

"Yes, sir, doubtless you will need it."

I struck a match and touched the candle-wick.

"Burglar?" said I. (For all my apparent coolness, my heart-beats were away up in the eighties!)

The girl snuggled close to my side. I could feel her heart beating even faster than mine.

"Burglar?" I repeated.

"Indeed, no, sir,"—reproachfully. "Mine is a political job."

"A political job?"—thunderstruck.

"Yes, sir; I am an inspector of cellars,"—grimly. "I couldn't get around to this here cellar earlier in the day, sir, and a fellow's work *must* be done."

Here was a burglar with the sense of humor.

"What can I do for you?" I asked blandly.

"Firstly, as they say, you might tell me what you and this lady *are* doing in this lonesome cellar."

"Say 'sir,' when you address me."

"Yes, sir."

"The lady and I were playing hide-and-seek."

"Nice game, sir,"—grinning. "Were you trying to hide under the coal?"

"Oh, no; I was merely exploring it."

"Say 'sir,' when you address me."

"Sir."

"You're a cool hand, sir."

"I am gratified to learn that our admiration is mutual. But what are *you* doing here?"

"I was ascertaining if the law was properly observed, sir," shaking with silent laughter.

"But what puzzles me," I went on, "is the fact that you could gather the gems in that garb." For I was positive that this was the Galloping Dick every one was looking for.

"I don't understand a word you say, sir. I'm an inspector of cellars, sir, not a jeweler. So you and the lady was playing hide-and-seek? Come, now, *what* is your graft? Is *all* the push here to-night?"

"That depends,"—cursing under my breath that I wore a gown which hampered my movements. For, truth to tell, I was watching him as a cat watches a mouse.

"Well, sir, we of the profession never interferes with gentlemanly jobs, sir. All I want of you is to help me out of here."

"I am not a burglar."

"Oh, I understand, sir; I understand completely. A gentleman is always a gentleman, sir. Now, you can return to that coal-bin. I was just about to make for it when you lit that candle."

"Why not leave by the cellar-doors?"

"I have my reasons, sir; most satisfactory reasons, sir. *I* prefer the window. Get along!"—his tones suddenly hardening.

I got along.

"The lady may sit down, sir," he said courteously.

"Thank you, I will," replied the girl, plumping down on an empty winecase. (She afterward confessed that if she had not sat down on the box, she would have sat down on the cellar-floor, as a sort of paralysis had seized her knees.)

I stepped into the coal-bin, and rested the candle on the little shelf for that purpose. I was downright anxious to see the fellow safely away. There wasn't room in that cellar for the three of us. His presence doubly endangered us and multiplied the complications. I was in no position to force the gems from him. A man who has ten thousand dollars' worth of jewels on his person doesn't stop at shooting; and I possessed a healthy regard for my skin. I opened the window and caught it to the ceiling by a hook I found there.

"There is a stout screen, my man."

"Take this, sir, and cut it out,"—handing me a pair of wire-clippers, holding his lantern under his arm meanwhile. The muzzle of the revolver, during all this time, never wavered in its aim at my head.

I went to work at the screen, and presently it fell inward.

"Is that satisfactory?"—with impressive irony.

"You are the most *perfect* gentleman that *I* ever see, sir!"

The girl laughed hysterically.

"Now what?" The fun was beginning to pall on me.

"Step out of the bin and stand aside. Sit down by the lady. Maybe she's a bit frightened."

I obeyed him to the letter.

"Thanks!" With the agility of a cat he leaped up and wriggled through the window. He turned. "Good night, sir. Sometime maybe I'll do the same for you, sir."

"Go to the devil!" I snarled.

"My, my! What a temper, sir! I wouldn't have thought it of you, and a nice lady in speaking distance!"

He disappeared.

The girl laid a hand on my arm.

"You have acted very sensibly, Mr. Comstalk. If you had not, it is quite certain he would have shot you."

"It would have been a good thing for me if he had. He has gone, and the jewels have gone with him. I hadn't the least chance; the wretch! He probably came disguised as a plumber, and nobody suspected him."

"But if he possessed the ten of hearts, why should he have left this way?"

"Possibly my idea was only an imitation of his. There must have been at least a dozen tens of hearts. My dear young lady, I would give a good deal if you were well out of this. I believed my plan was for the best, and instead I have simply blackened the case against us. I have been too adventurous. The situation looks very serious just now. Of course, in the long run, we shall clear ourselves; but it will take some fine arguing to do it, and possibly half a dozen lawyers."

"It is a terribly embarrassing predicament; but since we started out together, we'll hang together." She held out her hand to me. "It will be fun to extricate ourselves with full honors."

"You're a brick!" And I pressed her hand tightly.

"Now, I wonder why the burglar didn't try those cellar-doors?" she murmured.

"By Jove, I'll soon find out! Come on. There's hope yet."

This time we reached the stone steps without interference. I gave the candle to the girl, cautiously put a shoulder against one of the doors, and gave a gentle heave. It was not locked. Through the thin crack I looked out upon the bright world of moonshine and crystal. Instantly I permitted the door to settle into its accustomed place. I readily understood the burglar's reasons. Seated upon a box, less than a dozen feet away, and blissfully smoking one of the club's cigars, sat a burly policeman. So *they* had arrived upon the scene!

"What is it?" asked the girl, as I motioned her to retreat.

"The worst has come: the police!" dramatically.

"Gracious heavens, *this* is frightful! We shall never get out now. Oh dear! Why did I ever come? It will be in the papers, with horrid pictures. We ought not to have left the ball-room. Our very actions will tell heavily against us. Awful!"

"Now, don't you worry. They will not take any notice of you, once they set eyes upon me. *Homo sum*! They are looking for *me*. There's only one superfluous ten of hearts. I have it."

"But I shall be found with you, and the stupid police will swear I am an accomplice." She wrung her hands.

"But no jewels will be found upon us," I argued half-heartedly.

"They will say we have already disposed of them."

"But the real burglar—"

"They will say that he came into the cellar at our bidding."

This girl was terribly reasonable and direct.

"Hang it! I know Teddy Hamilton, the M. F. H. He'll go my bail, and yours, too, for that matter. Come, let's not give up. There *must* be some other way out."

"I wish I might believe it. Why *did* I come?"—a bit of a wail stealing into the anger in her voice.

"This is Tom Fool's Night, and no mistake," I assented ruefully.

"But I am a bigger fool than you are; I had an alibi, and a good one."

"An alibi? Why on earth, then, did you follow me? What is your alibi?"

"Never mind now. We should still be in this miserable cellar,"—briefly. "What a night! I am so ashamed! I shall be horribly compromised."

"I'll take the brunt of it all. I'm sorry; but, for the love of Heaven, don't cry, or I shall lose what little nerve I have left."

"I am not crying!" she denied emphatically. "My inclination is to shriek with laughter. I'm hysterical. And who wouldn't be, with police officers and cells staring one in the face? Let us be going. That policeman outside will presently hear us whispering if we stand here much longer."

There was wisdom in this. So, once again I took the candle, and we marched back. There wasn't a single jest left in my whole system, and it didn't look as if there was ever going to be another supply. We took the other side of the furnace, and at length came to a flight of wooden stairs, leading somewhere into the club. It was our last chance, or we should indeed be obliged to stay all night in some bin; for it would not be long before they searched the cellars. If this flight led into the kitchen, we were saved, for I could bluff the servants. We paused. Presently we ascended, side by side, with light but firm step. We reached the landing in front of the door without mishap. From somewhere came a puff of air which blew out the candle. I struck a match viciously against the wall—and blundered into a string of cooking-pans! It was all over, the agony of suspense!

Blang! Rumpity-bumpity-blang-blang!

I have heard many stage thunders in my time, but that racket beat anything and everything this side of siege-guns.

Instantly the door opened and a policeman poked his head in. Before I had time to move, he grabbed me by the arm and yanked me—into the ballroom! The girl and I had made a complete circuit of the cellars, and had stumbled into the ball-room again by the flight opposite to that by which we left it. Cheerful prospect, wasn't it? The adventure had ceased to have any droll side to it.

"Aha!" cried the base minion of the law. "*Here* you are, then! Hello, everybody! Hello!" he bawled.

Caught! Here we were, the Blue Domino and myself, the Grey Capuchin, both of us in a fine fix. Discovery and ejection I could have stood with fortitude and equanimity; but there was bad business afoot. There wasn't any doubt in my mind what was going to happen. As the girl said, there would be flaring head-lines and horrid pictures. We were like to be the newspaper sensation of the day. Arrested and lodged in jail! What would my rich, doting old uncle say to that, who had threatened to disinherit me for lesser things! I felt terribly sorry for the girl, but it was now utterly impossible to help her, for I couldn't help myself.

And behold! The mysterious stranger I had met in the curio-shop, the fellow who had virtually haunted me for six hours, the fellow who had masqueraded as Caesar, suddenly loomed up before me, still wearing his sardonic smile. At his side were two more policemen. He had thrown aside his toga and was in evening dress. His keen glance rested on me.

"Here he is, Mr. Haggerty!" cried the policeman cheerfully, swinging me around.

A detective! And Heaven help me, he believed me to be the thief! Oh, for Aladdin's lamp!

VI

I stood with folded arms, awaiting his approach. Nonchalance is always respected by the police. I must have presented a likely picture, however—my face blackened with coal-dust, cobwebs stringing down over my eyes, my Capuchin gown soiled and rent. The girl quietly took her place beside me.

"So you took a chance at the cellars, eh?" inquired the detective urbanely. "Well, you look it. Will you go with us quietly, or shall we have to use force?"

"In the first place, what do you and your police want of *me*?" I returned coolly.

He exhibited his star of authority.

"I am Haggerty of the Central Office. I want you for several things."

Several things? I stared at him stupidly. Several things? Then it came to me, with a jar like an earthquake. The story in the newspaper returned to my vision. Oh, this was too much, altogether too much! He took me to be the fashionable thief for whom half the New York police force were hunting. My sight swam for a moment in a blur.

"What is it you think I have done?" I demanded.

"You have, or have had, several thousand dollars' worth of gems on your person to-night."

I shrugged. The accusation was so impossible that my confidence returned.

"Mr. Haggerty, you are making a stupid mistake. You are losing time, besides. I am not the man for whom you are hunting. My name is Richard Comstalk."

"One name or another, it does not matter."

"Plenty of gall," murmured one of the minions of the law, whom I afterward learned was the chief of the village police.

"The card by which you gained admittance here," demanded the great Haggerty truculently.

I surrendered it. A crowd had by this time collected curiously about us. I could see the musicians on the stage peering over the plants.

"The thief you are looking for has gone," said I. "He escaped by the coal-window." By this statement, my feet sank deeper still.

"What did I tell you?" cried Haggerty, turning to his men. "They had an accomplice hidden in the cellars."

"I beg to inform you that you are making a mistake that will presently cost you dear,"—thinking of the political pull my uncle had in New York. "I am the nephew of Daniel Witherspoon."

"Worse and worse!" said the chief of police.

"We shall discuss the mistake later and at length. Of course you can easily explain how you came to impose upon these people,"—ironically. "Bah! the game is up. When you dropped that card in Friard's and said you were going to a masquerade, I knew your game in a minute, and laid eyes upon you for the first time since I began the chase. I've been after you for weeks. Your society dodge has worked out, and I'll land you behind the bars for some time to come, my gay boy. Come,"—roughly.

"I request Mr. Hamilton to be called. He will prove to you that you are greatly mistaken." Everything looked pretty black, I can tell you.

"You will see whom you please, but only after you are safely landed in the lockup. Now, Madame,"—turning swiftly upon the Blue Domino, "what is your part in this fine business?"

"It certainly has no part in yours,"—icily.

Haggerty smiled. "My skin is very thick. Do you know this fellow?"

She shook her head. He stood undecided for a space.

"Let me see your card."

"I decline to produce it,"—haughtily.

Haggerty seemed staggered for a moment. "I am sorry to annoy you, but you must be identified at once."

"And why?"—proudly. "Was it forbidden to go into the club cellars for such harmless things as apples?"

Apples! I looked at her admiringly.

"Apples?" repeated Haggerty. "Couldn't you have sent a servant for them?"

She did not reply.

"You were with this clever gentleman in the cellars. You may or may not be acquainted with him. I do not wish to do anything hasty in regard to yourself, but your position is rather equivocal. Produce your card and be identified—if you really can."

"I refuse!"

"Then I shall ask you to accompany us to the room up stairs till the police-patrol arrives."

"I will go,"—quietly.

"Nonsense!" I objected. "On my word of honor, I do not know this lady. Our presence in the cellar was perfectly harmless. There is no valid reason for detaining her. It is an outrage!"

"I am not going to stand here arguing with you," said Haggerty. "Let the lady produce her card; let her disclose her identity. That is simple enough."

"I have already given you my determination on that subject," replied the girl. "I can very well explain my presence here, but I absolutely decline to explain it to the police."

I didn't understand her at all. She had said that she possessed an alibi. Why didn't she produce it?

So the two of us left the gorgeous ball-room. Every one moved aside for us, and quickly, too, as if we had had the plague. I looked in vain for Hamilton. He was a friend in need. We were taken into the steward's office and the door was shut and locked. The band in the ball-room went galloping through a two-step, and the gaiety was in full swing again. The thief had been rounded up! How the deuce was it going to end?

"I can not tell you how sorry I am to have mixed you up in this," I said to the girl.

"You are in no manner to blame. Think of what *might* have happened had you blown up the post-office!"

She certainly was the least embarrassed of the two of us. I addressed my next remarks to the great Haggerty.

"Did you find a suitable pistol in Friard's?"

"A man in my business," said Haggerty mildly, "is often found in such places. There are various things to be recovered in pawnshops. The gentlemen of this club sent *me* the original ten of hearts, my presence being necessary at such big entertainments. And when I saw that card of yours, I was so happy that I nearly put you on your guard. Lord, how long I've been looking for you! I give you credit for being a clever rascal. You have fooled us all nicely. Not a soul among us knew your name, nor what you looked like. And but for that card, you might still be at large. Until the lady submits to the simple process of identification, I shall be compelled to look upon her and treat her as an accomplice. She has refused the offer I have made her, and she can not blame me if I am suspicious, when to be suspicious is a part of my business." He was reasonable enough in regard to the girl.

He turned to the chief of the village police, who was sitting at the desk ordinarily used by the club's steward.

"No reporters, mind you."

"Yes, sir. We'll see that no reporter gets wind of the capture."

The telephone bell rang. One of the police answered it.

"For you, Mr. Haggerty," he said.

Haggerty sprang to the telephone and placed the receiver to his ear.

"What?" we heard him exclaim. "You have got the other fellow? A horse and carriage at once!"

"Take mine," said the chief excitedly. "What is it?"

"My subordinate at the railway station has just landed the fellow with the jewels. Mighty quick work. I must hustle into town at once. There'll be plenty of time to attend to these persons. Bring them to town the moment the patrol arrives. The gems are the most important things just now."

"Yes, sir. You can rely upon us, Mr. Haggerty. Billy, go down with Mr. Haggerty and show him my rig."

"Good!" said Haggerty. "It's been a fine night's work, my lads, a fine night's work. I'll see that all get some credit. Permit no one to approach the prisoners without proper authority."

"Your orders shall be obeyed to the letter," said the chief importantly. He already saw his name figuring in the New York papers as having assisted in the capture of a great thief.

I cursed under my breath. If it hadn't been for the girl, I am ashamed to confess, I should have cursed out loud. She sat rigid and motionless. It must have been a cruel ordeal for her. But what was puzzling me was the fact that she made not the slightest effort to spring her alibi. If *I* had had one! Where was Hamilton? I scarcely inclined to the idea of sleeping in jail in a dress-suit.

Haggerty departed. A silence settled gloomily down on us. Quarter of an hour passed. The grim-visaged police watched us vigilantly. Half an hour, three-quarters, an hour. Far away we heard the whistle of an out-going train. Would I had been on it! From time to time we heard faint music. At length there was a noise outside the door, and a moment later Hamilton and two others came in. When he saw me, he stopped, his eyes bulging and his mouth agape.

"Dicky Comstalk?" he cried helplessly. "What the devil does this mean?"—turning to the police.

"Do you know this fellow, Mr. Hamilton?" asked the chief.

"Know him? Of course I know him," answered Teddy; "and I'll stake my last dollar on his honesty."

(Thanks, Teddy!) I began to breathe.

"But—" began the chief, seized with sudden misgivings.

"It is impossible, I tell you," interrupted Hamilton. "I know this gentleman is incapable of the theft. There is some frightful mistake. How the dickens did you get here, Dicky?"

And briefly I told him my story, my ass's ears growing inch by inch as I went along. Hamilton didn't know whether to swear or to laugh; finally he laughed.

"If you wanted to come, why didn't you write me for an invitation?"

"I shouldn't have come to your old ball, had I been invited. It was just the idea of the lark."

"We shall have to hold him, nevertheless," said the chief, "till everything is cleared up. The girl—"

Hamilton looked at the Blue Domino.

"Madame, will you do me the honor to raise your mask?"

She did so; and I

saw Hamilton draw in his breath. Her beauty was certainly of an exquisite pattern. He frowned anxiously.

"I never saw this young woman before," he admitted slowly.

"Ha!" cried the chief, glad to find some one culpable.

"Did you receive your invitation through the proper channels?" asked Hamilton.

"I came here to-night,"—coldly, "on the invitation of Mrs. Hyphen-Bonds, who sailed for Europe Wednesday."

Here was an alibi that was an alibi! I was all at sea. Hamilton bowed; the chief coughed worriedly behind his hand. The girl had told me she was an impostor like myself, that her ten of hearts was as dark-stained as my own. I could not make head or tail to it. Mrs. Hyphen-Bonds! She was a law in the land, especially in Blankshire, the larger part of which she owned. What did it all mean? And what was her idea in posing as an impostor?

The door opened again.

"The patrol has come," said the officer who entered.

"Let it wait," growled the chief. "Haggerty has evidently got us all balled up. I don't believe his fashionable thief has materialized at all; just a common crook. Well, he's got him, at any rate, and the gems."

"You have, of course, the general invitation?" said Hamilton.

"Here it is,"—and she passed the engraved card to him.

"I beg a thousand pardons!" said Hamilton humbly. "Everything seems to have gone wrong."

"Will you guarantee this man?" asked the chief of Hamilton, nodding toward me.

"I have said so. Mr. Comstalk is very well known to me. He is a retired army officer, and to my knowledge a man with an income sufficient to put him far beyond want."

"What is your name?" asked the chief of the girl, scowling. It was quite evident he couldn't understand her actions any better than I.

"Alice Hawthorne," with an oblique glance at me.

I had been right!

"What is your occupation? I am obliged to ask these questions, Miss."

"I am a miniature painter,"—briefly,

Hamilton came forward. "Alice Hawthorne? Pardon me, but are you the artist who recently completed the miniatures of the Emperor of Germany, the Princess of Hesse, and Mrs. Hyphen-Bonds?"

"I am. I believe there is no further reason for detaining me."

"Emperor of Germany?" echoed the now bewildered chief. "Why didn't you tell all this to Mr. Haggerty?"

"I had my reasons."

Once again the door opened. A burly man in a dark business-suit entered. His face ruddy and his little grey eyes sparkled with suppressed ire. He reminded me of Vautrin, the only difference being that Vautrin was French while this man was distinctly Irish. His massive shoulders betrayed tremendous strength. He was vastly angry about something. He went to the chief's desk and rested his hands upon it.

"You are a nice specimen for a chief of police, you are!" he began.

"And who the devil are *you*?" bawled the chief, his choler rising.

"I'll tell you who I am presently."

We all eyed him in wonder. What was going to happen now?

"Which of you gentlemen is Mr. Hamilton?" asked the new-comer gruffly.

Hamilton signified that he was the gentleman by that name.

"Some ladies at your ball have been robbed of their diamonds, I understand?"

"About ten thousand dollars' worth."

"Look here, sir," cried the chief, standing up and balling his fist, "I want you to explain yourself, and mighty quick. You can't come into my presence in this manner."

"Bah! You have just permitted the cleverest rascal in the state to slip through your butterfingers. *I* am Haggerty."

The chief of police sat down suddenly.

VII

The consummate daring of it! Why, the rascal ought to have been in command of an army. On the Board of Strategy he would have been incomparable!

There followed a tableau that I shall not soon forget. We all stared at the real Haggerty much after the fashion of Medusa's victims. Presently the tension relaxed, and we all sighed. I sighed because the thought of jail for the night in a dress-suit dwindled in perspective; the girl sighed for the same reason and one or two other things; the chief of the village police and his officers sighed because darkness had suddenly swooped down on them; and Hamilton sighed because there were no gems. Haggerty was the one among us who didn't sigh. He scowled blackly.

This big athlete looked like a detective, and the abrupt authority of his tones convinced me that he was. Haggerty was celebrated in the annals of police affairs; he had handled all sorts of criminals, from titled impostors down to petty thieves. He was not a man to trifle with, mentally or physically, and for this reason we were all shaking in our boots. He owned to a keen but brutal wit; to him there was no such thing as sex among criminals, and he had the tenacity of purpose that has given the bulldog considerable note in the pit. But it was quite plain that for once he had met his match.

"I don't see how you can blame me," mumbled the chief. "None of us was familiar with your looks, and he showed us his star of authority, and went to work in a business-like way—By George! and he has run away with my horse and carriage!"— starting from his chair.

"Never mind the horse. You'll find it safe at the railway station," snarled Haggerty. "Now, then, tell me everything that has happened, from beginning to end."

And the chief recounted the adventure briefly. Haggerty looked coldly at me and shrugged his broad shoulders. As for the girl, he never gave her so much as a single glance. He knew a gentlewoman without looking at her twice.

"Humph! Isn't he a clever one, though?" cried Haggerty, in a burst of admiration. "Clever is no name for it. I'd give a year of my life to come face to face with him. It would be an interesting encounter. Hunted him for weeks, and to-day laid eyes on him for the first time. Had my clumsy paws on him this very afternoon. He seemed so willing to be locked up that I grew careless. Biff! and he and his accomplice, an erstwhile valet, had me trussed like a chicken and bundled into the clothes-press. Took my star, credentials, playing-card, and invitation. It was near eleven o'clock when I roused the housekeeper. I telegraphed two hours ago."

"Telegraphed!" exclaimed the chief, rousing himself out of a melancholy dream. (There would be no mention of him in the morrow's papers.)

"Yes, telegraphed. The despatch lay unopened on your office-desk. You're a good watch-dog—for a hen-coop!" growled Haggerty. "Ten thousand in gems to-night, and by this time he is safe in New York. You are all a pack of blockheads.

"Used the telephone, did he? Told you to hold these innocent persons till he went somewhere to land the accomplice, eh? The whistle of the train meant nothing to you. Well, that whistle ought to have told you that there might be a mistake. A good officer never quits his prisoners. If there is an accomplice in toils elsewhere, he makes them bring him in, he does not go *out* for him. And now I've got to start all over again, and he in New York, a bigger catacomb than Rome ever boasted of. He's not a common thief; nobody knows who he is or what his haunts are. But I have seen his face; I'll never forget him."

The chief tore his hair, while his subordinates shuffled their feet uneasily. Then they all started in to explain their theories. But the detective silenced them with a wave of his huge hand.

"I don't want to hear any explanations. Let these persons go," he commanded, with a jerk of his head in our direction. "You can all return to town but one officer. I may need a single man," Haggerty added thoughtfully.

"What are you going to do?" asked the chief.

"Never you mind. I have an idea; it may be a good one. If it is, I'll telephone you all about it when the time comes."

He stepped over to the telephone and called up central. He spoke so low that none of us overheard what he said; but he hung up the receiver, a satisfied smile on his face.

The girl and I were free to go whither we listed, and we listed to return at once to New York. Hamilton, however, begged us to remain, to dance and eat, as a compensation for what we had gone through; but Miss Hawthorne resolutely shook her head; and as there was nothing in the world that would have induced me to stay without her, I shook my head, too. It seemed to me I had known this girl all my life, so closely does misfortune link one life to another. I had seen her for the first time less than eight hours before; and yet I was confident that as many years, under ordinary circumstances, would not have taught me her real worth.

"Mrs. Hyphen-Bonds will never forgive me," said Hamilton dismally, "if she hears that I've been the cause, indirectly and innocently, of turning you away."

"Mrs. Hyphen-Bonds need never know," replied the girl, smiling inscrutably. "In fact, it would be perfectly satisfactory and agreeable to me if she never heard at all."

"I will call a conveyance for you," said the defeated M. F. H. "I shall never forgive you, Dicky."

"Yes, you will, Teddy. A loving-cup, the next time we meet at the club, will mellow everything."

Quarter of an hour later Miss Hawthorne and I, wrapped in buffalo-robes, our feet snugly stowed away in straw, slid away, to the jangle and quarrel of sleighbells, toward Moriarty's Hollywood Inn. The moon shone; not a cloud darkened her serene and lovely countenance. The pearly whiteness of the world would have aroused the poetry in the most sordid soul; and far, far away to the east the black, tossing line of the sea was visible.

"What a beautiful night!" I volunteered.

"The beginning of the end."

"The beginning of the end? What does that mean?"

"Why, when you first spoke to me, it was about the weather."

"Oh, but this isn't going to be the end; this is the true beginning of all things."

"I wish I could see it in that light; but we can not see beauty in anything when hunger lies back of the eyes. I haven't had anything to eat, save that single apple, for hours and hours. I was so excited at Mouquin's that I ate almost nothing."

"You are hungry? Well, we'll fix that when we get to Moriarty's. I'll find a way of waking him up, in case he's asleep, which I doubt. There will be cold chicken and ham and hot coffee."

"Lovely!"

"And we shall dine with the gods. And now it is all over and done, it *was* funny, wasn't it?"

"Terribly funny!"—with a shade of irony. "It would have been funnier still if the real Haggerty hadn't turned up. The patrol had arrived."

"But it didn't happen. I shall never forget this night,"— romantically.

"I should be inordinately glad to forget it completely,"— decidedly.

"Where's your romance?" I asked.

"I'd rather have it served to me between book-covers. As I grow older my love of repose increases."

"Do you know," I began boldly, "it seems that I have known you all my life."

"Indeed!"

"Yes. Why, I might really have known you all my life, and still not have known you as well as I do this very minute,—and less than a dozen hours between this and our first meeting. You are as brave as a paladin, wise as a serpent, cool, witty—and beautiful!"

"Shall I ask the driver to let me out?" Then she laughed, a rollicking, joyous laugh.

"What is so funny?"

"I was thinking of that coal-bin."

"Well, I didn't permit a lonely potato to frighten me," I retorted.

"No, you were brave enough—among the potatoes."

"You *are* beautiful!"

"I am hungry."

"You are the most beautiful girl—"

"I want something to eat."

"—I ever saw! Do you think it possible for a man to fall in love at first sight?"

"Oh, nothing is impossible on Tom Fool's night. Positive, fool; comparative, fooler; superlative, foolest. You are marching on with your degrees, Mr. Comstalk."

"You might call me Dicky," I said in an aggrieved tone.

"Dicky? Never! I should always be thinking of paper collars."

"I wish *I* were witty like that!"

She snuggled down beneath the robes.

An artist's model, thought I. Never in this world. I now understood the drift of her uncle's remark about her earning capacity. The Alice Hawthorne miniatures brought fabulous prices. And here I was, sitting so close to her that our shoulders touched: and she a girl who knew intimately emperors and princesses and dukes, not to mention the worldly-rich. I admit that for a moment I was touched with awe. And it was beginning to get serious. This girl interested me marvelously. I summoned up all my courage.

"Are—are you married?"

"No-o."

"Nor engaged to be married?"

"No-o. But you mustn't ask all these questions."

"How would you like to ride around in a first-class motor-car the rest of your days?"

She laughed merrily. Possibly it *was* funny.

"Are you always amusing like this?"

"Supposing I were serious?"

"In that case I should say you had not yet slipped off your fool's motley."

This directness was discouraging.

"I wonder if the ten of hearts is lucky, after all," I mused.

"We are not in jail. I consider that the best of good fortune."

"Give me your card," said I.

She gave me the card, and I put it with mine.

"Why do you do that?"

"Perhaps I want to bring about an enchantment,"—soberly.

"As Signor Fantoccini, or as Mr. Comstalk?"

"I have long since resigned my position in the museum; it was too exciting."

She made no rejoinder; and for some time there was no sound but the music of the bells.

Finally we drew up under the colonial porte-cochere of Hollywood Inn and were welcomed by the genial Moriarty himself, his Celtic countenance a mirror of smiles.

"Anything in the house to eat?" I cried, shaking the robes from me.

"Anything ye like, if you like cowld things. I can hate ye a pot of coffee on the gasolene-burner, and there's manny a vintage in the cillars."

"That will be plenty!"—joyfully, helping Miss Hawthorne to alight.

"Sure, and ye are from the Hunt Club!"—noting our costumes. "Well, well! They niver have anny too much grub. Now, I'll putt ye in a little room all be yersilves, with a windy and a log-fire; cozy as ye plaze. Ye'll have nearly two hours to wait for the car-r from the village."

We entered the general assembly-room. It was roomy and quaint, and somewhere above us was the inevitable room in which George Washington had slept. The great hooded fireplace was merry with crackling logs. Casually I observed that we were not alone. Over yonder, in a shadowed corner, sat two men, very well bundled up, and, to all appearances, fast asleep. Moriarty lighted a four-branched candelabrum and showed us the way to the little private dining-room, took our orders, and left us.

"This is romance," said I. "They used to do these things hundreds of years ago, and everybody had a good time."

"It is now all very wicked and improper," murmured the girl, laying aside her domino for the first time; "but delightful! I now find I haven't the least bit of remorse for what I have done."

In that dark evening gown she was very beautiful. Her arms and shoulders were tinted like Carrara marble; and I knew instantly that I was never going to recover. I drew two chairs close to the grate. I sat down in one and she in the other. With a contented sigh she rested her blue-slippered feet on the brass fender.

"My one regret is that I haven't any shoes. What an adventure!"

"It's fine!" Two hours in the society of this enchanting creature! It was almost too good to be true. Ah, if it might always be like this—to return home from the day's work, to be greeted warmly by a woman as beautiful as this one! I sighed loudly.

Moriarty came with the chicken and ham and coffee.

"If ye would like, it won't be a bit of trouble to show ye George Washington's room; or"—with inimitable Irish drollery—"I can tell ye that he dined in this very room."

"That will serve," smiled the girl; and Moriarty bowed himself out.

His departure was followed by the clatter of silver upon porcelain. Of a truth, both of us were hungry.

"I was simply ravenous," the girl confessed.

"And as for me, I never dreamt I could be so unromantic. Now," said I, pushing aside my plate, and dropping sugar into my coffee, and vainly hunting in my pockets for a cigar, "there remains only one mystery to be cleared up."

"And what might this mystery be?" she asked. "The whereabouts of the bogus Haggerty?"

"The bogus Haggerty will never cross our paths again. He has skipped by the light of the moon. No, that's not the mystery. Why did you tell me you were an impostor; why did you go to the cellars with me, when all the while you were at the ball on Mrs. Hyphen-Bonds' invitation?"

She leaned on her elbows and smiled at me humorously.

"Would you really like to know, Signor? Well, I was an impostor." She sat with her back to the fire, and a weird halo of light seemed to surround her and frame her. "Mrs. Hyphen-Bonds accidentally dropped that invitation in my studio, a few days before she sailed for Europe. I simply could not resist the temptation. That is all the mystery there is."

"And they still think you were there rightfully!"

"You are no longer mystified?"

"Yes; there is yet another mystery to solve: myself." I knew it. Without rhyme or reason, I was in love; and without rhyme or reason, I was glad of it.

"Shall you ever be able to solve such a mystery?"— quizzically.

"It all depends upon you."

"Mr. Comstalk, you will not mar the exquisite humor of our adventure by causing me any annoyance. I am sure that some day we shall be very good friends. But one does not talk of love on eight hours' acquaintance. Besides, you would be taking advantage of my helplessness; for I really depend upon you to see me safe back to New York. It is only the romance, the adventure; and such moonlight nights often superinduce sentimentality. What do you know of me? Nothing. What do I know of you? Nothing, save that there is a kindred spirit which is always likely to lead us into trouble. Down in your heart you know you are only temporarily affected by moonshine. Come, make me a toast!"—lifting her cup.

"You are right," said I. "I am a gentleman. But it was only consistent that, having been the fool, I should now play the ass. Here's!"—and I held up my cup.

But neither of us drank; there wasn't time.

For the door opened quietly, and in walked the two men we had seen upon entering the Inn. One of them gently closed the door and locked it. One was in soiled every-day clothes, the other in immaculate evening dress. The latter doffed his opera hat with the most engaging smile imaginable. The girl and I looked up at him in blank bewilderment, and set our cups down so mechanically that the warm amber liquid spattered on the table-cloth.

Galloping Dick and the affable inspector of the cellars stood before us!

VIII

"The unexpected always happens," began the pseudo-detective, closing his hat, drawing off his gloves and stuffing them into a pocket. "As a friend of mine used to say, it is the unexpected that always surprises us. We never expected to see these charming masqueraders again, did we, William?"

"No, sir," said William, grinning affably, "we didn't. The gentleman was very nice and obliging to me, sir, when I was in the cellars."

"So I understand. Now," continued the late Mr. Haggerty, with the deadly affability of a Macaire, "I beg of you, Mr. Comstalk, I beg of you not to move or to become unduly excited. Physicians tell us that excitement wastes the red corpuscles, that is to say, the life of the blood."

"Your blood, sir, must be very thin," I returned coolly. But I cursed him soundly in my mind. William's bulging side-pocket convinced me that any undue excitement on my part would be exceedingly dangerous.

"William, you can always tell a gentleman," said the chief rogue admiringly. "A gentleman always recognizes his opportunities, and never loses his sense of the balance of things."

"And he is usually witty, too, sir," William assented.

The girl sat pale and rigid in her chair.

"What do you want?" I demanded savagely.

"For one thing, I should like to question the propriety of a gentleman's sitting down to dine with a lady without having washed his face. The coal-dust does not add to your manly beauty. You haven't a cake of soap about you, William, have you?"

"No, sir." William's face expressed indescribable enjoyment of the scene.

The girl's mouth stiffened. She was struggling to repress the almost irresistible smile that tickled her lips.

"In times like these," said I, determined not to be outdone, "we are often thoughtless in regard to our personal appearances. I apologize to the lady."

"Fine, fine! I sincerely admire you, Mr. Comstalk. You have the true spirit of adventure. Hasn't he, William?"

"He certainly has, sir."

"Comes to a private ball without an invitation, and has a merry time of it indeed. To have the perfect sense of humor—that is what makes the world go round."

"Aren't you taking extra risk in offering me these pleasantries?" I asked.

"Risks? In what manner?"

"The man you so cleverly impersonated is at the club." I do not know what prompted me to put him on his guard.

The rogue laughed lightly. "I know Mr. Haggerty's habits. He is hustling back to New York as fast as he can. He passed here ten minutes ago in the patrol, lickety-clip! He wishes to warn all pawnbrokers and jewelers to be on the lookout for me to-morrow. Ten thousand in a night!"—jovially.

"A *very* tidy sum, sir," said William.

"A fourth of which goes to you, my good and faithful friend."

"Thank you, sir," replied William.

Two cooler rogues I never wish to meet!

"But wouldn't it be well, sir, to hasten?" asked William.

"We have plenty of time now, my son."

"You have not entered this room," said the girl, her terror slipping from her, "simply to offer these banalities. What do you wish?"

"What perspicacity, William!" cried the rogue, taking out a cigarette case.

"I don't know what that word means, sir, but as you do, it seems to fit the occasion proper enough."

"It means, William, that this charming young lady scents our visit from afar."

"I had a suspicion, sir, that it might mean that." William leaned against the wall, his beady eyes twinkling merrily.

The master rogue lighted a cigarette at one of the candles.

"Pardon me," he said, "but will you join me?"—proffering the handsome gold case.

I took a cigarette and fired it. (I really wanted it.) I would show up well before this girl if I died for it. I blew a cloud of smoke at the candle-flame. There *was* a sparkle of admiration in the girl's eyes.

"Mr. Comstalk, my respect for you increases each moment." The rogue sat down.

"And to whom might this handsome case belong?" I asked, examining it closely.

"Oh, that has always been mine. There was a time,"—blowing rings at the candelabrum,—"when I was respected like yourself, rich, sought after. A woman and a trusted friend: how these often tumble down our beautiful edifices! Yes, I am a scamp, a thief, a rogue; but not because I need the money. No,"—with retrospective eyes—"I need excitement, tremendous and continuous,—excitement to keep my vigilance and invention active day and night, excitement to obliterate memory.

"But we can't do it, my friend, we can't do it. Memory is always with us. She is an impartial Nemesis; she dogs the steps of the righteous and the unrighteous. To obliterate memory, that is it! And where might I find this obliteration, save in this life? Drugs? Pah! Oh, I have given Haggerty a royal chase. It has been meat and drink to me to fool the cleverest policeman in New York. Till yesterday my face, as a criminal, was unknown to any man or woman, save William here, who was my valet in the old days. I have gone to my clubs, dined, played billiards; a fine comedy, a fine comedy! To-morrow William and I sail for Europe. Miss Hawthorne, you wear one of the most exquisite rubies I have ever seen. Permit me to examine it."

The girl tore the ring from her finger and flung it on the table. I made a move as though to push back my chair.

"I wouldn't do it, sir," warned William quietly.

My muscles relaxed.

"Do not commit any rash action, Mr. Comstalk," said the girl, smiling bravely into my eyes. "This gentleman would not appreciate it."

The master rogue picked up the ring and rolled it lovingly about his palms.

"Beautiful, beautiful!" he murmured. "Finest pigeon-blood, too. It is easily worth a thousand. Shall I give you my note of exchange for it?"—humorously. The girl scorned to reply. He took out a little chamois bag and emptied its contents on the table. How they sparkled, scintillated, glowed; thousands in the whitest of stones! How he ever had got his fingers on them is something I shall never learn. "Aren't they just beautiful?" he asked naively. "Can you blame me for coveting them?" He set the ruby on top of the glittering heap. It lay there like a drop of blood. Presently he caught it up and—presented it to the girl, who eyed him in astonishment. "I only wanted to look at it," he said courteously. "I like your grit as much as I admire your beauty. Keep the ring."

She slipped it mechanically over her finger.

"But you, my dear Mr. Comstalk!" he cried, turning his shining eyes upon me, while his fingers deftly replaced the gems in the bag.

"I have no jewelry," I replied, tossing aside the cigarette.

"But you have something infinitely better. I am rather observant. In Friard's curio-shop you carelessly exhibited a wallet that was simply choking to death with long yellow-boys. You have it still. Will you do me the honor?"—stretching out his slim white hand.

I looked at William; he nodded. There wasn't the slightest chance for me to argue. So I drew out my wallet. I extracted the gold-bills and made a neat little packet of them. It hurt, hurt like the deuce, to part with them. But—!

"Game, William, isn't he? Most men would have flung the wallet at my head."

"Oh, he is game, sir; never you doubt it, sir," said the amiable William.

"I have some silver in change," I suggested with some bitterness.

"Far be it that I should touch silver," he said generously, did this rogue. "Besides, you will need something to pay for this little supper and the fare back to New York." My bills disappeared into his pocket. "You will observe that I trust you implicitly. I haven't even counted the money."

William sniggered.

"And is there anything further?" I inquired. The comedy was beginning to weary me, it was so one-sided.

"I am in no particular hurry," the rogue answered, his sardonic smile returning. "It is so long since I have chatted with people of my kind."

I scowled.

"Pardon me, I meant from a social point of view only. I admit we would not be equals in the eye of the Presbyter."

And then followed a scene that reminds me to this day of some broken, fantastic dream, a fragment from some bewildering nightmare.

IX

For suddenly I saw his eyes widen and flash with anger and apprehension. Quick as a passing sunshadow, his hand swept the candelabrum from the table. He made a swift backward spring toward the door, but he was a little too late. The darkness he had created was not intense enough, for there was still the ruddy glow from the logs; and the bosom of his dress-shirt made a fine target. Besides, the eyes that had peered into the window were accustomed to the night.

Blang! The glass of the window shivered and jingled to the floor, and a sharp report followed. The rogue cried out in fierce anguish, and reeled against the wall. William whipped out his revolver, but, even from his favorable angle, he was not quick enough. The hand that had directed the first bullet was ready to direct the second.

All this took place within the count of ten. The girl and I sat stiffly in our chairs, as if petrified, it was all so swiftly accomplished.

"Drop it!" said a cold, authoritative voice, and I saw the vague outlines of Haggerty's face beyond the broken window-pane.

William knew better than to hesitate. His revolver struck the floor dully, and a curse rolled from his lips. Immediately a heavy body precipitated itself against the door, which crashed inward, and an officer fearlessly entered, a revolver in each hand. This tableau, which lasted fully a minute, was finally disturbed by the entrance of Haggerty himself.

"Don't be alarmed, Miss," he said heartily; "it's all over, I'm sorry for the bullet, but it had to be done. The rascal has nothing more serious than a splintered bone, I am a dead shot. A fine night!"—triumphantly. "It's been a long chase, and I never was sure of the finish. You're the cleverest rogue it has been my good fortune to meet this many a day. I don't even know who you are yet. Well, well! we'll round that up in time."

Not till the candles again sputtered with light, and William was securely handcuffed and disarmed, did I recollect that I possessed the sense of motion. The smoke of powder drifted across the flickering candles, and there was a salty taste on my tongue.

"Horrible!" cried the girl, covering her eyes.

The master rogue and his valet were led out into the assembly-room, and we reluctantly followed. I saw it all now. When Haggerty called up central at the club, he ascertained where the last call had been from, and, learning that it came from Hollywood Inn, he took his chance. The room was soon filled with servants and stable-hands, the pistol-shot having lured them from their beds. The wounded man was very pale. He sat with his uninjured hand tightly clasped above the ragged wound, and a little pool of blood slowly formed at his side on the floor. But his eyes shone brightly.

"A basin of water and some linen!" cried the girl to Moriarty. "And send all these people away."

"To yer rooms, ivery one of ye!" snapped Moriarty, sweeping his hands. "'Tis no place for ye, be off!" He hurried the servants out of the room, and presently returned with a basin of water, some linen and balm.

We watched the girl as she bathed and bandaged the wounded arm; and once or twice the patient smiled. Haggerty looked on approvingly, and in William's eyes there beamed the gentle light of reverence. It *was* a picture to see this lovely creature playing the part of the good Samaritan, moving here and there in her exquisite gown. Ah, the tender mercy! I knew that, come what might, I had strangely found the right woman, the one woman.

"You're a good little woman," said the rogue, his face softening; "and a good woman is the finest thing God ever placed upon earth. Had I only found one!" He turned whimsically toward me. "Are you engaged to marry this little woman?"

"No."

"Surely you love her!"

"Surely I do!" I looked bravely at the girl as I spoke.

But she never gave any sign that she heard. She pinned the ends of the bandages carefully.

"And what brought you to this?" asked Haggerty, looking down at his prisoner.

The prisoner shrugged.

"You've the making of a fine man in you," went on Haggerty generously. "What caused you to slip up?"

"That subject is taboo," replied the thief. "But I want to beg your pardon for underestimating your cunning."

"It was all due to a chance shot at the telephone."

"I kept you guessing."

"Merrily, too. My admiration is wholly yours, sir," returned Haggerty, picking up the telephone exchange-book. He rang and placed his lips to the transmitter, calling a number. "Hello! Is this the chief of the Blankshire police? Yes? Well, this is Haggerty. That idea I hinted to you was a mighty good one. Prepare two strong cells and have a doctor on hand. What? Oh, you will find your horse and carriage at Moriarty's. Good-by!"

My money was handed over to me. I returned it to my wallet, but without any particular enthusiasm.

"It's a bad business, William," said I.

"It's all in the game, sir,"—with a look at Haggerty that expressed infinite hatred. "In our business we can't afford to be careless."

"Or to talk too much," supplemented his master, smiling. "Talk, my friend, rounds me up with a bullet in the arm, and a long sojourn behind stone walls. Never talk. Thank you, Miss Hawthorne, and you, too, Mr. Comstalk, for the saving grace of humor. If it were possible, I should like to give Miss Hawthorne the pick of the jewels. This is a sordid world."

"Ye'er car-r is coming!" shouted Moriarty, running to the window.

So the girl and I passed out of Hollywood Inn, leaving Haggerty with his mysterious prisoners. I can't reason it out, even to this day, but I was genuinely sorry that Haggerty had arrived upon the scene. For one thing, he had spoiled the glamour of the adventure by tingeing it with blood. And on the way to the car I wondered what had been the rogue's past, what had turned him into this hardy, perilous path. He had spoken of a woman; perhaps that was it. They are always behind good actions and bad. Heigh-ho!

Once we were seated in the lonely car, the girl broke down and cried as if her heart would break. It was only the general reaction, but the sight of her tears unnerved me.

"Don't cry, girl; don't!" I whispered, taking her hand in mine. She made no effort to repulse me. "I am sorry. The rascal was a gallant beggar, and I for one shouldn't have been sorry to see him get away. There, there! You're the bravest, tenderest girl in all this world; and when I told him I loved you, God knows I meant it! It is one of those inexplicable things. You say I have known you only eight hours? I have known you always, only I had not met you. What are eight hours? What is convention, formality? We two have lived a lifetime in these eight hours. Can't you see that we have?"

"To shoot a human being!" she sobbed. Her head fell against my shoulder. I do not believe she was conscious of the fact. And I did not care a hang for the conductor.

I patted her hand encouragingly. "It had to be done. He was in a desperate predicament, and he would have shot Haggerty had the detective been careless in has turn; and he wouldn't have aimed to maim, either."

"What a horrible night! It will haunt me as long as I live!"

I said nothing; and we did not speak again till the first of the Blankshire lights flashed by us. By this time her sobs had ceased.

"I know I haven't done anything especially gallant to-night; no fighting, no rescuing, and all that. They just moved *me* around like a piece of stage scenery."

A smile flashed and was gone. It was a hopeful sign.

"But the results are the same. You have admitted to me that you are neither engaged nor married. Won't you take me on—on approval?"

"Mr. Comstalk, it all seems so like a horrid dream. You *are* a brave man, and what is better, a sensible one, for you submitted to the inevitable with the best possible grace. But you talk of love as readily as a hero in a popular novel."

"I never go back," said I. "It seems incredible, doesn't it, that I should declare myself in this fashion? Listen. For my part, I believe that all this was written,—my Tom-foolery in Mouquin's, my imposture and yours, the two identical cards,—the adventure from beginning to end."

Silence.

"Suppose I should say," the girl began, looking out of the window, "that in the restaurant you aroused my curiosity, that in the cellars my admiration was stirred, that the frank manner in which you expressed your regard for me to—to the burglar— awakened—"

"What?" I cried eagerly.

"Nothing. It was merely a supposition."

"Hang it; I *do* love you!"

"Are you still the Capuchin, or simply Mr. Comstalk?"

"I have laid aside all masks, even that which hides the heart."

She turned and looked me steadily in the eyes.

"Well?" said I.

"If I took you on—on approval, what in the world should I do with you in case you should not suit my needs?"

"You could return me," said I laughing.

But she didn't.

THE AFFAIR AT THE SEMIRAMIS HOTEL
BY A.E.W. MASON

ORIGINALLY PUBLISHED IN 1917

THE AFFAIR AT THE SEMIRAMIS HOTEL
BY A.E.W. MASON

A.E.W. Mason's tale features one of the original odd couples of detective fiction, the very French Inspector Hanaud, and the just as British retired financier, Mr. Ricardo. This pair was originally introduced in the novel *At the Villa Rose*, and were to go on to feature in four other novels. Here they make an appearance in the shorter but no less worthy "The Affair at the Semiramis Hotel."

That these two very different personalities can cooperate at all is surprising, that they have become fast friends is astounding. Hanaud is said to have been modeled on two actual heads of the Paris Surete, Mason and Goron, as well as the fictional Lecoq, and is said to have influenced Agatha Christie. He is stout, broad-shouldered, he lives and investigates with a Gallic flair, and has an appreciation of good food and wine. Mr. Ricardo is reserved, correct, apt to reach the wrong conclusions, but he serves as a perfect foil for the French detective.

The story itself involves a mysterious murder, an even more mysterious woman, and a string of stolen pearls. It is convoluted and intricate, and perhaps a little more serious than the other two stories in this collection. Yet it is told with the same sort of wit as its companions and is equally entertaining.

About the Author

Alfred Edward Woodley Mason (May 7, 1865-November 22, 1948) was a London born author and politician. His career outside of writing included being a member of parliament and serving with British Naval Intelligence during World War I. As an author, he wrote over twenty books and three successful plays. His most famous work is *The Four Feathers* which has been made into several films. He also wrote the series of books featuring the French detective Inspector Hanaud whom he introduced in *At the Villa Rose*.

THE AFFAIR AT THE
SEMIRAMIS HOTEL

I

Mr. Ricardo, when the excitements of the Villa Rose were done with, returned to Grosvenor Square and resumed the busy, unnecessary life of an amateur. But the studios had lost their savour, artists their attractiveness, and even the Russian opera seemed a trifle flat. Life was altogether a disappointment; Fate, like an actress at a restaurant, had taken the wooden pestle in her hand and stirred all the sparkle out of the champagne; Mr. Ricardo languished—until one unforgettable morning.

He was sitting disconsolately at his breakfast-table when the door was burst open and a square, stout man, with the blue, shaven face of a French comedian, flung himself into the room. Ricardo sprang towards the new-comer with a cry of delight.

"My dear Hanaud!"

He seized his visitor by the arm, feeling it to make sure that here, in flesh and blood, stood the man who had introduced him to the acutest sensations of his life. He turned towards his butler, who was still bleating expostulations in the doorway at the unceremonious irruption of the French detective.

"Another place, Burton, at once," he cried, and as soon as he and Hanaud were alone: "What good wind blows you to London?"

"Business, my friend. The disappearance of bullion somewhere on the line between Paris and London. But it is finished. Yes, I take a holiday."

A light had suddenly flashed in Mr. Ricardo's eyes, and was now no less suddenly extinguished. Hanaud paid no attention whatever to his friend's disappointment. He pounced upon a piece of silver which adorned the tablecloth and took it over to the window.

"Everything is as it should be, my friend," he exclaimed, with a grin. "Grosvenor Square, the *Times* open at the money column, and a false antique upon the table. Thus I have dreamed of you. All Mr. Ricardo is in that sentence."

Ricardo laughed nervously. Recollection made him wary of Hanaud's sarcasms. He was shy even to protest the genuineness of his silver. But, indeed, he had not the time. For the door opened again and once more the butler appeared. On this occasion, however, he was alone.

"Mr. Calladine would like to speak to you, sir," he said.

"Calladine!" cried Ricardo in an extreme surprise. "That is the most extraordinary thing." He looked at the clock upon his mantelpiece. It was barely half-past eight. "At this hour, too?"

"Mr. Calladine is still wearing evening dress," the butler remarked.

Ricardo started in his chair. He began to dream of possibilities; and here was Hanaud miraculously at his side.

"Where is Mr. Calladine?" he asked.

"I have shown him into the library."

"Good," said Mr. Ricardo. "I will come to him."

But he was in no hurry. He sat and let his thoughts play with this incident of Calladine's early visit.

"It is very odd," he said. "I have not seen Calladine for months—no, nor has anyone. Yet, a little while ago, no one was more often seen."

He fell apparently into a muse, but he was merely seeking to provoke Hanaud's curiosity. In this attempt, however, he failed. Hanaud continued placidly to eat his breakfast, so that Mr. Ricardo was compelled to volunteer the story which he was burning to tell.

"Drink your coffee, Hanaud, and you shall hear about Calladine."

Hanaud grunted with resignation, and Mr. Ricardo flowed on:

"Calladine was one of England's young men. Everybody said so. He was going to do very wonderful things as soon as he had made up his mind exactly what sort of wonderful things he was going to do. Meanwhile, you met him in Scotland, at Newmarket, at Ascot, at Cowes, in the box of some great lady at the Opera— not before half-past ten in the evening *there*—in any fine house where the candles that night happened to be lit. He went everywhere, and then a day came and he went nowhere. There was no scandal, no trouble, not a whisper against his good name. He simply vanished. For a little while a few people asked: 'What has become of Calladine?' But there never was any answer, and London has no time for unanswered questions. Other promising young men dined in his place. Calladine had joined the huge legion of the Come-to-nothings. No one even seemed to pass him in the street. Now unexpectedly, at half-past eight in the morning, and in evening dress, he calls upon me. 'Why?' I ask myself."

Mr. Ricardo sank once more into a reverie. Hanaud watched him with a broadening smile of pure enjoyment.

"And in time, I suppose," he remarked casually, "you will perhaps ask him?"

Mr. Ricardo sprang out of his pose to his feet.

"Before I discuss serious things with an acquaintance," he said with a scathing dignity, "I make it a rule to revive my impressions of his personality. The cigarettes are in the crystal box."

"They would be," said Hanaud, unabashed, as Ricardo stalked from the room. But in five minutes Mr. Ricardo came running back, all his composure gone.

"It is the greatest good fortune that you, my friend, should have chosen this morning to visit me," he cried, and Hanaud nodded with a little grimace of resignation.

"There goes my holiday. You shall command me now and always. I will make the acquaintance of your young friend."

He rose up and followed Ricardo into his study, where a young man was nervously pacing the floor.

"Mr. Calladine," said Ricardo. "This is Mr. Hanaud."

The young man turned eagerly. He was tall, with a noticeable elegance and distinction, and the face which he showed to Hanaud was, in spite of its agitation, remarkably handsome.

"I am very glad," he said. "You are not an official of this country. You can advise—without yourself taking action, if you'll be so good."

Hanaud frowned. He bent his eyes uncompromisingly upon Calladine.

"What does that mean?" he asked, with a note of sternness in his voice.

"It means that I must tell someone," Calladine burst out in quivering tones. "That I don't know what to do. I am in a difficulty too big for me. That's the truth."

Hanaud looked at the young man keenly. It seemed to Ricardo that he took in every excited gesture, every twitching feature, in one comprehensive glance. Then he said in a friendlier voice:

"Sit down and tell me"—and he himself drew up a chair to the table.

"I was at the Semiramis last night," said Calladine, naming one of the great hotels upon the Embankment. "There was a fancy-dress ball."

All this happened, by the way, in those far-off days before the war—nearly, in fact, three years ago today—when London, flinging aside its reticence, its shy self-consciousness, had become a city of carnivals and masquerades, rivalling its neighbours on the Continent in the spirit of its gaiety, and exceeding them by its stupendous luxury. "I went by the merest chance. My rooms are in the Adelphi Terrace."

"There!" cried Mr. Ricardo in surprise, and Hanaud lifted a hand to check his interruptions.

"Yes," continued Calladine. "The night was warm, the music floated through my open windows and stirred old memories. I happened to have a ticket. I went."

Calladine drew up a chair opposite to Hanaud and, seating himself, told, with many nervous starts and in troubled tones, a story which, to Mr. Ricardo's thinking, was as fabulous as any out of the "Arabian Nights."

"I had a ticket," he began, "but no domino. I was consequently stopped by an attendant in the lounge at the top of the staircase leading down to the ballroom.

"'You can hire a domino in the cloakroom, Mr. Calladine,' he said to me. I had already begun to regret the impulse which had brought me, and I welcomed the excuse with which the absence of a costume provided me. I was, indeed, turning back to the door, when a girl who had at that moment run down from the stairs of the hotel into the lounge, cried gaily: 'That's not necessary'; and at the same moment she flung to me a long scarlet cloak which she had been wearing over her own dress. She was young, fair, rather tall, slim, and very pretty; her hair was drawn back from her face with a ribbon, and rippled down her shoulders in heavy curls; and she was dressed in a satin coat and knee-breeches of pale green and gold, with a white waistcoat and silk stockings and scarlet heels to her satin shoes. She was as straight-limbed as a boy, and exquisite like a figure in Dresden china. I caught the cloak and turned to thank her. But she did not wait. With a laugh she ran down the stairs a supple and shining figure, and was lost in the throng at the doorway of the ballroom. I was stirred by the prospect of an adventure. I ran down after her. She was standing just inside the room alone, and she was gazing at the scene with parted lips and dancing eyes. She laughed again as she saw the cloak about my shoulders, a delicious gurgle of amusement, and I said to her:

"'May I dance with you?'

"'Oh, do!' she cried, with a little jump, and clasping her hands. She was of a high and joyous spirit and not difficult in the matter of an introduction. 'This gentleman will do very well to present us,' she said, leading me in front of a bust of the God Pan which stood in a niche of the wall. 'I am, as you see, straight out of an opera. My name is Celymene or anything with an eighteenth century sound to it. You are—what you will. For this evening we are friends.'

"'And for to-morrow?' I asked.

"'I will tell you about that later on,' she replied, and she began to dance with a light step and a passion in her dancing which earned me many an envious glance from the other men. I was in luck, for Celymene knew no one, and though, of course, I saw the faces of a great many people whom I remembered, I kept them all at a distance. We had been dancing for about half an hour when the first queerish thing happened. She stopped suddenly in the midst of a sentence with a little gasp. I spoke to her, but she did not hear. She was gazing past me, her eyes wide open, and such a rapt look upon her face as I had never seen. She was lost in a miraculous vision. I followed the direction of her eyes and, to my astonishment, I saw nothing more than a stout, short, middle-aged woman, egregiously over-dressed as Marie Antoinette.

"'So you do know someone here?' I said, and I had to repeat the words sharply before my friend withdrew her eyes. But even then she was not aware of me. It was as if a voice had spoken to her whilst she was asleep and had disturbed, but not wakened her. Then she came to—there's really no other word I can think of which describes her at that moment—she came to with a deep sigh.

"'No,' she answered. 'She is a Mrs. Blumenstein from Chicago, a widow with ambitions and a great deal of money. But I don't know her.'

"'Yet you know all about her,' I remarked.

"'She crossed in the same boat with me,' Celymene replied. 'Did I tell you that I landed at Liverpool this morning? She is staying at the Semiramis too. Oh, let us dance!'

"She twitched my sleeve impatiently, and danced with a kind of violence and wildness as if she wished to banish some sinister thought. And she did undoubtedly banish it. We supped together and grew confidential, as under such conditions people will. She told me her real name. It was Joan Carew.

"'I have come over to get an engagement if I can at Covent Garden. I am supposed to sing all right. But I don't know anyone. I have been brought up in Italy.'

"'You have some letters of introduction, I suppose?' I asked.

"'Oh, yes. One from my teacher in Milan. One from an American manager.'

"In my turn I told her my name and where I lived, and I gave her my card. I thought, you see, that since I used to know a good many operatic people, I might be able to help her.

"'Thank you,' she said, and at that moment Mrs. Blumenstein, followed by a party, chiefly those lap-dog young men who always seem to gather about that kind of person, came into the supper-room and took a table close to us. There was at once an end of all confidences—indeed, of all conversation. Joan Carew lost all the lightness of her spirit; she talked at random, and her eyes were drawn again and again to the grotesque slander on Marie Antoinette. Finally I became annoyed.

"'Shall we go?' I suggested impatiently, and to my surprise she whispered passionately:

"'Yes. Please! Let us go.'

"Her voice was actually shaking, her small hands clenched. We went back to the ballroom, but Joan Carew did not recover her gaiety, and half-way through a dance, when we were near to the door, she stopped abruptly—extraordinarily abruptly.

"'I shall go,' she said abruptly. 'I am tired. I have grown dull.'

"I protested, but she made a little grimace.

"'You'll hate me in half an hour. Let's be wise and stop now while we are friends,' she said, and whilst I removed the domino from my shoulders she stooped very quickly. It seemed to me that she picked up something which had lain hidden beneath the sole of her slipper. She certainly moved her foot, and I certainly saw something small and bright flash in the palm of her glove as she raised herself again. But I imagined merely that it was some object which she had dropped.

"'Yes, we'll go,' she said, and we went up the stairs into the lobby. Certainly all the sparkle had gone out of our adventure. I recognized her wisdom.

"'But I shall meet you again?' I asked.

"'Yes. I have your address. I'll write and fix a time when you will be sure to find me in. Good-night, and a thousand thanks. I should have been bored to tears if you hadn't come without a domino.'

"She was speaking lightly as she held out her hand, but her grip tightened a little and—clung. Her eyes darkened and grew troubled, her mouth trembled. The shadow of a great trouble had suddenly closed about her. She shivered.

"'I am half inclined to ask you to stay, however dull I am; and dance with me till daylight—the safe daylight,' she said.

"It was an extraordinary phrase for her to use, and it moved me.

"'Let us go back then!' I urged. She gave me an impression suddenly of someone quite forlorn. But Joan Carew recovered her courage. 'No, no,' she answered quickly. She snatched her hand away and ran lightly up the staircase, turning at the corner to wave her hand and smile. It was then half-past one in the morning."

So far Calladine had spoken without an interruption. Mr. Ricardo, it is true, was bursting to break in with the most important questions, but a salutary fear of Hanaud restrained him. Now, however, he had an opportunity, for Calladine paused.

"Half-past one," he said sagely. "Ah!"

"And when did you go home?" Hanaud asked of Calladine.

"True," said Mr. Ricardo. "It is of the greatest consequence."

Calladine was not sure. His partner had left behind her the strangest medley of sensations in his breast. He was puzzled, haunted, and charmed. He had to think about her; he was a trifle uplifted; sleep was impossible. He wandered for a while about the ballroom. Then he walked to his chambers along the echoing streets and sat at his window; and some time afterwards the hoot of a motor-horn broke the silence and a car stopped and whirred in the street below. A moment later his bell rang.

He ran down the stairs in a queer excitement, unlocked the street door and opened it. Joan Carew, still in her masquerade dress with her scarlet cloak about her shoulders, slipped through the opening.

"Shut the door," she whispered, drawing herself apart in a corner.

"Your cab?" asked Calladine.

"It has gone."

Calladine latched the door. Above, in the well of the stairs, the light spread out from the open door of his flat. Down here all was dark. He could just see the glimmer of her white face, the glitter of her dress, but she drew her breath like one who has run far. They mounted the stairs cautiously. He did not say a word until they were both safely in his parlour; and even then it was in a low voice.

"What has happened?"

"You remember the woman I stared at? You didn't know why I stared, but any girl would have understood. She was wearing the loveliest pearls I ever saw in my life."

Joan was standing by the edge of the table. She was tracing with her finger a pattern on the cloth as she spoke. Calladine started with a horrible presentiment.

"Yes," she said. "I worship pearls. I always have done. For one thing, they improve on me. I haven't got any, of course. I have no money. But friends of mine who do own pearls have sometimes given theirs to me to wear when they were going sick, and they have always got back their lustre. I think that has had a little to do with my love of them. Oh, I have always longed for them—just a little string. Sometimes I have felt that I would have given my soul for them."

She was speaking in a dull, monotonous voice. But Calladine recalled the ecstasy which had shone in her face when her eyes first had fallen on the pearls, the longing which had swept her quite into another world, the passion with which she had danced to throw the obsession off.

"And I never noticed them at all," he said.

"Yet they were wonderful. The colour! The lustre! All the evening they tempted me. I was furious that a fat, coarse creature like that should have such exquisite things. Oh, I was mad."

She covered her face suddenly with her hands and swayed. Calladine sprang towards her. But she held out her hand.

"No, I am all right." And though he asked her to sit down she would not. "You remember when I stopped dancing suddenly?"

"Yes. You had something hidden under your foot?"

The girl nodded.

"Her key!" And under his breath Calladine uttered a startled cry.

For the first time since she had entered the room Joan Carew raised her head and looked at him. Her eyes were full of terror, and with the terror was mixed an incredulity as though she could not possibly believe that that had happened which she knew had happened.

"A little Yale key," the girl continued. "I saw Mrs. Blumenstein looking on the floor for something, and then I saw it shining on the very spot. Mrs. Blumenstein's suite was on the same floor as mine, and her maid slept above. All the maids do. I knew that. Oh, it seemed to me as if I had sold my soul and was being paid."

Now Calladine understood what she had meant by her strange phrase—"the safe daylight."

"I went up to my little suite," Joan Carew continued. "I sat there with the key burning through my glove until I had given her time enough to fall asleep"—and though she hesitated before she spoke the words, she did speak them, not looking at Calladine, and with a shudder of remorse making her confession complete. "Then I crept out. The corridor was dimly lit. Far away below the music was throbbing. Up here it was as silent as the grave. I opened the door—her door. I found myself in a lobby. The suite, though bigger, was arranged like mine. I slipped in and closed the door behind me. I listened in the darkness. I couldn't hear a sound. I crept forward to the door in front of me. I stood with my fingers on the handle and my heart beating fast enough to choke me. I had still time to turn back. But I couldn't. There were those pearls in front of my eyes, lustrous and wonderful. I opened the door gently an inch or so—and then—it all happened in a second."

Joan Carew faltered. The night was too near to her, its memory too poignant with terror. She shut her eyes tightly and cowered down in a chair. With the movement her cloak slipped from her shoulders and dropped on to the ground. Calladine leaned forward with an exclamation of horror; Joan Carew started up.

"What is it?" she asked.

"Nothing. Go on."

"I found myself inside the room with the door shut behind me. I had shut it myself in a spasm of terror. And I dared not turn round to open it. I was helpless."

"What do you mean? She was awake?"

Joan Carew shook her head.

"There were others in the room before me, and on the same errand—men!"

Calladine drew back, his eyes searching the girl's face.

"Yes?" he said slowly.

"I didn't see them at first. I didn't hear them. The room was quite dark except for one jet of fierce white light which beat upon the door of a safe. And as I shut the door the jet moved swiftly and the light reached me and stopped. I was blinded. I stood in the full glare of it, drawn up against the panels of the door, shivering, sick with fear. Then I heard a quiet laugh, and someone moved softly towards me. Oh, it was terrible! I recovered the use of my limbs; in a panic I turned to the door, but I was too late. Whilst I fumbled with the handle I was seized; a hand covered my mouth. I was lifted to the centre of the room. The jet went out, the electric lights were turned on. There were two men dressed as apaches in velvet trousers and red scarves, like a hundred others in the ballroom below, and both were masked. I struggled furiously; but, of course, I was like a child in their grasp. 'Tie her legs,' the man whispered who was holding me; 'she's making too much noise.' I kicked and fought, but the other man stooped and tied my ankles, and I fainted."

Calladine nodded his head.

"Yes?" he said.

"When I came to, the lights were still burning, the door of the safe was open, the room empty; I had been flung on to a couch at the foot of the bed. I was lying there quite free."

"Was the safe empty?" asked Calladine suddenly.

"I didn't look," she answered. "Oh!"—and she covered her face spasmodically with her hands. "I looked at the bed. Someone was lying there—under a sheet and quite still. There was a clock ticking in the room; it was the only sound. I was terrified. I was going mad with fear. If I didn't get out of the room at once I felt that I should go mad, that I should scream and bring everyone to find me alone with—what was under the sheet in the bed. I ran to the door and looked out through a slit into the corridor. It was still quite empty, and below the music still throbbed in the ballroom. I crept down the stairs, meeting no one until I reached the hall. I looked into the ballroom as if I was searching for someone. I stayed long enough to show myself. Then I got a cab and came to you."

A short silence followed. Joan Carew looked at her companion in appeal. "You are the only one I could come to," she added. "I know no one else."

Calladine sat watching the girl in silence. Then he asked, and his voice was hard:

"And is that all you have to tell me?"

"Yes."

"You are quite sure?"

Joan Carew looked at him perplexed by the urgency of his question. She reflected for a moment or two.

"Quite."

Calladine rose to his feet and stood beside her.

"Then how do you come to be wearing this?" he asked, and he lifted a chain of platinum and diamonds which she was wearing about her shoulders. "You weren't wearing it when you danced with me."

Joan Carew stared at the chain.

"No. It's not mine. I have never seen it before." Then a light came into her eyes. "The two men—they must have thrown it over my head when I was on the couch—before they went." She looked at it more closely. "That's it. The chain's not very valuable. They could spare it, and—it would accuse me—of what they did."

"Yes, that's very good reasoning," said Calladine coldly.

Joan Carew looked quickly up into his face.

"Oh, you don't believe me," she cried. "You think—oh, it's impossible." And, holding him by the edge of his coat, she burst into a storm of passionate denials.

"But you went to steal, you know," he said gently, and she answered him at once:

"Yes, I did, but not this." And she held up the necklace. "Should I have stolen this, should I have come to you wearing it, if I had stolen the pearls, if I had"—and she stopped—"if my story were not true?"

Calladine weighed her argument, and it affected him.

"No, I think you wouldn't," he said frankly.

Most crimes, no doubt, were brought home because the criminal had made some incomprehensibly stupid mistake; incomprehensibly stupid, that is, by the standards of normal life. Nevertheless, Calladine was inclined to believe her. He looked at her. That she should have murdered was absurd. Moreover, she was not making a parade of remorse, she was not playing the unctuous penitent; she had yielded to a temptation, had got herself into desperate straits, and was at her wits' ends how to escape from them. She was frank about herself.

Calladine looked at the clock. It was nearly five o'clock in the morning, and though the music could still be heard from the ballroom in the Semiramis, the night had begun to wane upon the river.

"You must go back," he said. "I'll walk with you."

They crept silently down the stairs and into the street. It was only a step to the Semiramis. They met no one until they reached the Strand. There many, like Joan Carew in masquerade, were standing about, or walking hither and thither in search of carriages and cabs. The whole street was in a bustle, what with drivers shouting and people coming away.

"You can slip in unnoticed," said Calladine as he looked into the thronged courtyard. "I'll telephone to you in the morning."

"You will?" she cried eagerly, clinging for a moment to his arm.

"Yes, for certain," he replied. "Wait in until you hear from me. I'll think it over. I'll do what I can."

"Thank you," she said fervently.

He watched her scarlet cloak flitting here and there in the crowd until it vanished through the doorway. Then, for the second time, he walked back to his chambers, while the morning crept up the river from the sea.

* * * * *

This was the story which Calladine told in Mr. Ricardo's library. Mr. Ricardo heard it out with varying emotions. He began with a thrill of expectation like a man on a dark threshold of great excitements. The setting of the story appealed to him, too, by a sort of brilliant bizarrerie which he found in it. But, as it went on, he grew puzzled and a trifle disheartened. There were flaws and chinks; he began to bubble with unspoken criticisms, then swift and clever thrusts which he dared not deliver. He looked upon the young man with disfavour, as upon one who had half opened a door upon a theatre of great promise and shown him a spectacle not up to the mark. Hanaud, on the other hand, listened imperturbably, without an expression upon his face, until the end. Then he pointed a finger at Calladine and asked him what to Ricardo's mind was a most irrelevant question.

"You got back to your rooms, then, before five, Mr. Calladine, and it is now nine o'clock less a few minutes."

"Yes."

"Yet you have not changed your clothes. Explain to me that. What did you do between five and half-past eight?"

Calladine looked down at his rumpled shirt front.

"Upon my word, I never thought of it," he cried. "I was worried out of my mind. I couldn't decide what to do. Finally, I determined to talk to Mr. Ricardo, and after I had come to that conclusion I just waited impatiently until I could come round with decency."

Hanaud rose from his chair. His manner was grave, but conveyed no single hint of an opinion. He turned to Ricardo.

"Let us go round to your young friend's rooms in the Adelphi," he said; and the three men drove thither at once.

II

Calladine lodged in a corner house and upon the first floor. His rooms, large and square and lofty, with Adams mantelpieces and a delicate tracery upon their ceilings, breathed the grace of the eighteenth century. Broad high windows, embrasured in thick walls, overlooked the river and took in all the sunshine and the air which the river had to give. And they were furnished fittingly. When the three men entered the parlour, Mr. Ricardo was astounded. He had expected the untidy litter of a man run to seed, the neglect and the dust of the recluse. But the room was as clean as the deck of a yacht; an Aubusson carpet made the floor luxurious underfoot; a few coloured prints of real value decorated the walls; and the mahogany furniture was polished so that a lady could have used it as a mirror. There was even by the newspapers upon the round table a china bowl full of fresh red roses. If Calladine had turned hermit, he was a hermit of an unusually fastidious type. Indeed, as he stood with his two companions in his dishevelled dress he seemed quite out of keeping with his rooms.

"So you live here, Mr. Calladine?" said Hanaud, taking off his hat and laying it down.

"Yes."

"With your servants, of course?"

"They come in during the day," said Calladine, and Hanaud looked at him curiously.

"Do you mean that you sleep here alone?"

"Yes."

"But your valet?"

"I don't keep a valet," said Calladine; and again the curious look came into Hanaud's eyes.

"Yet," he suggested gently, "there are rooms enough in your set of chambers to house a family."

Calladine coloured and shifted uncomfortably from one foot to the other.

"I prefer at night not to be disturbed," he said, stumbling a little over the words. "I mean, I have a liking for quiet."

Gabriel Hanaud nodded his head with sympathy.

"Yes, yes. And it is a difficult thing to get—as difficult as my holiday," he said ruefully, with a smile for Mr. Ricardo.

"However"—he turned towards Calladine—"no doubt, now that you are at home, you would like a bath and a change of clothes. And when you are dressed, perhaps you will telephone to the Semiramis and ask Miss Carew to come round here. Meanwhile, we will read your newspapers and smoke your cigarettes."

Hanaud shut the door upon Calladine, but he turned neither to the papers nor the cigarettes. He crossed the room to Mr. Ricardo, who, seated at the open window, was plunged deep in reflections.

"You have an idea, my friend," cried Hanaud. "It demands to express itself. That sees itself in your face. Let me hear it, I pray."

Mr. Ricardo started out of an absorption which was altogether assumed.

"I was thinking," he said, with a faraway smile, "that you might disappear in the forests of Africa, and at once everyone would be very busy about your disappearance. You might leave your village in Leicestershire and live in the fogs of Glasgow, and within a week the whole village would know your postal address. But London—what a city! How different! How indifferent! Turn out of St. James's into the Adelphi Terrace and not a soul will say to you: 'Dr. Livingstone, I presume?'"

"But why should they," asked Hanaud, "if your name isn't Dr. Livingstone?"

Mr. Ricardo smiled indulgently.

"Scoffer!" he said. "You understand me very well," and he sought to turn the tables on his companion. "And you—does this room suggest nothing to you? Have you no ideas?" But he knew very well that Hanaud had. Ever since Hanaud had crossed the threshold he had been like a man stimulated by a drug. His eyes were bright and active, his body alert.

"Yes," he said, "I have."

He was standing now by Ricardo's side with his hands in his pockets, looking out at the trees on the Embankment and the barges swinging down the river.

"You are thinking of the strange scene which took place in this room such a very few hours ago," said Ricardo. "The girl in her masquerade dress making her confession with the stolen chain about her throat——"

Hanaud looked backwards carelessly. "No, I wasn't giving it a thought," he said, and in a moment or two he began to walk about the room with that curiously light step which Ricardo was never able to reconcile with his cumbersome figure. With the heaviness of a bear he still padded. He went from corner to corner, opened a cupboard here, a drawer of the bureau there, and—stooped suddenly. He stood erect again with a small box of morocco leather in his hand. His body from head to foot seemed to Ricardo to be expressing the question, "Have I found it?" He pressed a spring and the lid of the box flew open. Hanaud emptied its contents into the palm of his hand. There were two or three sticks of sealing-wax and a seal. With a shrug of the shoulders he replaced them and shut the box.

"You are looking for something," Ricardo announced with sagacity.

"I am," replied Hanaud; and it seemed that in a second or two he found it. Yet—yet—he found it with his hands in his pockets, if he had found it. Mr. Ricardo saw him stop in that attitude in front of the mantelshelf, and heard him utter a long, low whistle. Upon the mantelshelf some photographs were arranged, a box of cigars stood at one end, a book or two lay between some delicate ornaments of china, and a small engraving in a thin gilt frame was propped at the back against the wall. Ricardo surveyed the shelf from his seat in the window, but he could not imagine which it was of these objects that so drew and held Hanaud's eyes.

Hanaud, however, stepped forward. He looked into a vase and turned it upside down. Then he removed the lid of a porcelain cup, and from the very look of his great shoulders Ricardo knew that he had discovered what he sought. He was holding something in his hands, turning it over, examining it. When he was satisfied he moved swiftly to the door and opened it cautiously. Both men could hear the splashing of water in a bath. Hanaud closed the door again with a nod of contentment and crossed once more to the window.

"Yes, it is all very strange and curious," he said, "and I do not regret that you dragged me into the affair. You were quite right, my friend, this morning. It is the personality of your young Mr. Calladine which is the interesting thing. For instance, here we are in London in the early summer. The trees out, freshly green, lilac and flowers in the gardens, and I don't know what tingle of hope and expectation in the sunlight and the air. I am middle-aged—yet there's a riot in my blood, a recapture of youth, a belief that just round the corner, beyond the reach of my eyes, wonders wait for me. Don't you, too, feel something like that? Well, then—" and he heaved his shoulders in astonishment.

"Can you understand a young man with money, with fastidious tastes, good-looking, hiding himself in a corner at such a time—except for some overpowering reason? No. Nor can I. There is another thing—I put a question or two to Calladine."

"Yes," said Ricardo.

"He has no servants here at night. He is quite alone and—here is what I find interesting—he has no valet. That seems a small thing to you?" Hanaud asked at a movement from Ricardo. "Well, it is no doubt a trifle, but it's a significant trifle in the case of a young rich man. It is generally a sign that there is something strange, perhaps even something sinister, in his life. Mr. Calladine, some months ago, turned out of St. James's into the Adelphi. Can you tell me why?"

"No," replied Mr. Ricardo. "Can you?"

Hanaud stretched out a hand. In his open palm lay a small round hairy bulb about the size of a big button and of a colour between green and brown.

"Look!" he said. "What is that?"

Mr. Ricardo took the bulb wonderingly.

"It looks to me like the fruit of some kind of cactus."

Hanaud nodded.

"It is. You will see some pots of it in the hothouses of any really good botanical gardens. Kew has them, I have no doubt. Paris certainly has. They are labelled. 'Anhalonium Luinii.' But amongst the Indians of Yucatan the plant has a simpler name."

"What name?" asked Ricardo.

"Mescal."

Mr. Ricardo repeated the name. It conveyed nothing to him whatever.

"There are a good many bulbs just like that in the cup upon the mantelshelf," said Hanaud.

Ricardo looked quickly up.

"Why?" he asked.

"Mescal is a drug."

Ricardo started.

"Yes, you are beginning to understand now," Hanaud continued, "why your young friend Calladine turned out of St. James's into the Adelphi Terrace."

Ricardo turned the little bulb over in his fingers.

"You make a decoction of it, I suppose?" he said.

"Or you can use it as the Indians do in Yucatan," replied Hanaud. "Mescal enters into their religious ceremonies. They sit at night in a circle about a fire built in the forest and chew it, whilst one of their number beats perpetually upon a drum."

Hanaud looked round the room and took notes of its luxurious carpet, its delicate appointments. Outside the window there was a thunder in the streets, a clamour of voices. Boats went swiftly down the river on the ebb. Beyond the mass of the Semiramis rose the great grey-white dome of St. Paul's. Opposite, upon the Southwark bank, the giant sky-signs, the big Highlander drinking whisky, and the rest of them waited, gaunt skeletons, for the night to limn them in fire and give them life. Below the trees in the gardens rustled and waved. In the air were the uplift and the sparkle of the young summer.

"It's a long way from the forests of Yucatan to the Adelphi Terrace of London," said Hanaud. "Yet here, I think, in these rooms, when the servants are all gone and the house is very quiet, there is a little corner of wild Mexico."

A look of pity came into Mr. Ricardo's face. He had seen more than one young man of great promise slacken his hold and let go, just for this reason. Calladine, it seemed, was another.

"It's like bhang and kieff and the rest of the devilish things, I suppose," he said, indignantly tossing the button upon the table.

Hanaud picked it up.

"No," he replied. "It's not quite like any other drug. It has a quality of its own which just now is of particular importance to you and me. Yes, my friend"—and he nodded his head very seriously—"we must watch that we do not make the big fools of ourselves in this affair."

"There," Mr. Ricardo agreed with an ineffable air of wisdom, "I am entirely with you."

"Now, why?" Hanaud asked. Mr. Ricardo was at a loss for a reason, but Hanaud did not wait. "I will tell you. Mescal intoxicates, yes—but it does more—it gives to the man who eats of it colour-dreams."

"Colour-dreams?" Mr. Ricardo repeated in a wondering voice.

"Yes, strange heated charms, in which violent things happen vividly amongst bright colours. Colour is the gift of this little prosaic brown button." He spun the bulb in the air like a coin, and catching it again, took it over to the mantelpiece and dropped it into the porcelain cup.

"Are you sure of this?" Ricardo cried excitedly, and Hanuad raised his hand in warning. He went to the door, opened it for an inch or so, and closed it again.

"I am quite sure," he returned. "I have for a friend a very learned chemist in the College de France. He is one of those enthusiasts who must experiment upon themselves. He tried this drug."

"Yes," Ricardo said in a quieter voice. "And what did he see?"

"He had a vision of a wonderful garden bathed in sunlight, an old garden of gorgeous flowers and emerald lawns, ponds with golden lilies and thick yew hedges—a garden where peacocks stepped indolently and groups of gay people fantastically dressed quarrelled and fought with swords. That is what he saw. And he saw it so vividly that, when the vapours of the drug passed from his brain and he waked, he seemed to be coming out of the real world into a world of shifting illusions."

Hanaud's strong quiet voice stopped, and for a while there was a complete silence in the room. Neither of the two men stirred so much as a finger. Mr. Ricardo once more was conscious of the thrill of strange sensations. He looked round the room. He could hardly believe that a room which had been—nay was—the home and shrine of mysteries in the dark hours could wear so bright and innocent a freshness in the sunlight of the morning. There should be something sinister which leaped to the eyes as you crossed the threshold.

"Out of the real world," Mr. Ricardo quoted. "I begin to see."

"Yes, you begin to see, my friend, that we must be very careful not to make the big fools of ourselves. My friend of the College de France saw a garden. But had he been sitting alone in the window-seat where you are, listening through a summer night to the music of the masquerade at the Semiramis, might he not have seen the ballroom, the dancers, the scarlet cloak, and the rest of this story?"

"You mean," cried Ricardo, now fairly startled, "that Calladine came to us with the fumes of mescal still working in his brain, that the false world was the real one still for him."

"I do not know," said Hanaud. "At present I only put questions. I ask them of you. I wish to hear how they sound. Let us reason this problem out. Calladine, let us say, takes a great deal more of the drug than my professor. It will have on him a more powerful effect while it lasts, and it will last longer. Fancy dress balls are familiar things to Calladine. The music floating from the Semiramis will revive old memories. He sits here, the pageant takes shape before him, he sees himself taking his part in it. Oh, he is happier here sitting quietly in his window-seat than if he was actually at the Semiramis. For he is there more intensely, more vividly, more really, than if he had actually descended this staircase. He lives his story through, the story of a heated brain, the scene of it changes in the way dreams have, it becomes tragic and sinister, it oppresses him with horror, and in the morning, so obsessed with it that he does not think to change his clothes, he is knocking at your door."

Mr. Ricardo raised his eyebrows and moved.

"Ah! You see a flaw in my argument," said Hanaud. But Mr. Ricardo was wary. Too often in other days he had been leaped upon and trounced for a careless remark.

"Let me hear the end of your argument," he said. "There was then to your thinking no temptation of jewels, no theft, no murder—in a word, no Celymene? She was born of recollections and the music of the Semiramis."

"No!" cried Hanaud. "Come with me, my friend. I am not so sure that there was no Celymene."

With a smile upon his face, Hanaud led the way across the room. He had the dramatic instinct, and rejoiced in it. He was going to produce a surprise for his companion and, savouring the moment in advance, he managed his effects. He walked towards the mantelpiece and stopped a few paces away from it.

"Look!"

Mr. Ricardo looked and saw a broad Adams mantelpiece. He turned a bewildered face to his friend.

"You see nothing?" Hanaud asked.

"Nothing!"

"Look again! I am not sure—but is it not that Celymene is posing before you?"

Mr. Ricardo looked again. There was nothing to fix his eyes. He saw a book or two, a cup, a vase or two, and nothing else really expect a very pretty and apparently valuable piece of— and suddenly Mr. Ricardo understood. Straight in front of him, in the very centre of the mantelpiece, a figure in painted china was leaning against a china stile. It was the figure of a perfectly impossible courtier, feminine and exquisite as could be, and apparelled also even to the scarlet heels exactly as Calladine had described Joan Carew.

Hanaud chuckled with satisfaction when he saw the expression upon Mr. Ricardo's face.

"Ah, you understand," he said. "Do you dream, my friend? At times—yes, like the rest of us. Then recollect your dreams? Things, people, which you have seen perhaps that day, perhaps months ago, pop in and out of them without making themselves prayed for. You cannot understand why. Yet sometimes they cut their strange capers there, logically, too, through subtle associations which the dreamer, once awake, does not apprehend. Thus, our friend here sits in the window, intoxicated by his drug, the music plays in the Semiramis, the curtain goes up in the heated theatre of his brain. He sees himself step upon the stage, and who else meets him but the china figure from his mantelpiece?"

Mr. Ricardo for a moment was all enthusiasm. Then his doubt returned to him.

"What you say, my dear Hanaud, is very ingenious. The figure upon the mantelpiece is also extremely convincing. And I should be absolutely convinced but for one thing."

"Yes?" said Hanaud, watching his friend closely.

"I am—I may say it, I think, a man of the world. And I ask myself"—Mr. Ricardo never could ask himself anything without assuming a manner of extreme pomposity—"I ask myself, whether a young man who has given up his social ties, who has become a hermit, and still more who has become the slave of a drug, would retain that scrupulous carefulness of his body which is indicated by dressing for dinner when alone?"

Hanaud struck the table with the palm of his hand and sat down in a chair.

"Yes. That is the weak point in my theory. You have hit it. I knew it was there—that weak point, and I wondered whether you would seize it. Yes, the consumers of drugs are careless, untidy—even unclean as a rule. But not always. We must be careful. We must wait."

"For what?" asked Ricardo, beaming with pride.

"For the answer to a telephone message," replied Hanaud, with a nod towards the door.

Both men waited impatiently until Calladine came into the room. He wore now a suit of blue serge, he had a clearer eye, his skin a healthier look; he was altogether a more reputable person. But he was plainly very ill at ease. He offered his visitors cigarettes, he proposed refreshments, he avoided entirely and awkwardly the object of their visit. Hanaud smiled. His theory was working out. Sobered by his bath, Calladine had realised the foolishness of which he had been guilty.

"You telephone, to the Semiramis, of course?" said Hanaud cheerfully.

Calladine grew red.

"Yes," he stammered.

"Yet I did not hear that volume of 'Hallos' which precedes telephonic connection in your country of leisure," Hanaud continued.

"I telephoned from my bedroom. You would not hear anything in this room."

"Yes, yes; the walls of these old houses are solid." Hanaud was playing with his victim. "And when may we expect Miss Carew?"

"I can't say," replied Calladine. "It's very strange. She is not in the hotel. I am afraid that she has gone away, fled."

Mr. Ricardo and Hanaud exchanged a look. They were both satisfied now. There was no word of truth in Calladine's story.

"Then there is no reason for us to wait," said Hanaud. "I shall have my holiday after all." And while he was yet speaking the voice of a newsboy calling out the first edition of an evening paper became distantly audible. Hanaud broke off his farewell. For a moment he listened, with his head bent. Then the voice was heard again, confused, indistinct; Hanaud picked up his hat and cane and, without another word to Calladine, raced down the stairs. Mr. Ricardo followed him, but when he reached the pavement, Hanaud was half down the little street. At the corner, however, he stopped, and Ricardo joined him, coughing and out of breath.

"What's the matter?" he gasped.

"Listen," said Hanaud.

At the bottom of Duke Street, by Charing Cross Station, the newsboy was shouting his wares. Both men listened, and now the words came to them mispronounced but decipherable.

"Mysterious crime at the Semiramis Hotel."

Ricardo stared at his companion.

"You were wrong then!" he cried. "Calladine's story was true."

For once in a way Hanaud was quite disconcerted.

"I don't know yet," he said. "We will buy a paper."

But before he could move a step a taxi-cab turned into the Adelphi from the Strand, and wheeling in front of their faces, stopped at Calladine's door. From the cab a girl descended.

"Let us go back," said Hanaud.

III

Mr. Ricardo could no longer complain. It was half-past eight when Calladine had first disturbed the formalities of his house in Grosvenor Square. It was barely ten now, and during that short time he had been flung from surprise to surprise, he had looked underground on a morning of fresh summer, and had been thrilled by the contrast between the queer, sinister life below and within and the open call to joy of the green world above. He had passed from incredulity to belief, from belief to incredulity, and when at last incredulity was firmly established, and the story to which he had listened proved the emanation of a drugged and heated brain, lo! the facts buffeted him in the face, and the story was shown to be true.

"I am alive once more," Mr. Ricardo thought as he turned back with Hanaud, and in his excitement he cried his thought aloud.

"Are you?" said Hanaud. "And what is life without a newspaper? If you will buy one from that remarkably raucous boy at the bottom of the street I will keep an eye upon Calladine's house till you come back."

Mr. Ricardo sped down to Charing Cross and brought back a copy of the fourth edition of the *Star*. He handed it to Hanaud, who stared at it doubtfully, folded as it was.

"Shall we see what it says?" Ricardo asked impatiently.

"By no means," Hanaud answered, waking from his reverie and tucking briskly away the paper into the tail pocket of his coat. "We will hear what Miss Joan Carew has to say, with our minds undisturbed by any discoveries. I was wondering about something totally different."

"Yes?" Mr. Ricardo encouraged him. "What was it?"

"I was wondering, since it is only ten o'clock, at what hour the first editions of the evening papers appear."

"It is a question," Mr. Ricardo replied sententiously, "which the greatest minds have failed to answer."

And they walked along the street to the house. The front door stood open during the day like the front door of any other house which is let off in sets of rooms. Hanaud and Ricardo went up the staircase and rang the bell of Calladine's door. A middle-aged woman opened it.

"Mr. Calladine is in?" said Hanaud.

"I will ask," replied the woman. "What name shall I say?"

"It does not matter. I will go straight in," said Hanaud quietly. "I was here with my friend but a minute ago."

He went straight forward and into Calladine's parlour. Mr. Ricardo looked over his shoulder as he opened the door and saw a girl turn to them suddenly a white face of terror, and flinch as though already she felt the hand of a constable upon her shoulder. Calladine, on the other hand, uttered a cry of relief.

"These are my friends," he exclaimed to the girl, "the friends of whom I spoke to you"; and to Hanaud he said: "This is Miss Carew."

Hanaud bowed.

"You shall tell me your story, mademoiselle," he said very gently, and a little colour returned to the girl's cheeks, a little courage revived in her.

"But you have heard it," she answered.

"Not from you," said Hanaud.

So for a second time in that room she told the history of that night. Only this time the sunlight was warm upon the world, the comfortable sounds of life's routine were borne through the windows, and the girl herself wore the inconspicuous blue serge of a thousand other girls afoot that morning. These trifles of circumstance took the edge of sheer horror off her narrative, so that, to tell the truth, Mr. Ricardo was a trifle disappointed. He wanted a crescendo motive in his music, whereas it had begun at its fortissimo. Hanaud, however, was the perfect listener. He listened without stirring and with most compassionate eyes, so that Joan Carew spoke only to him, and to him, each moment that passed, with greater confidence. The life and sparkle of her had gone altogether. There was nothing in her manner now to suggest the waywardness, the gay irresponsibility, the radiance, which had attracted Calladine the night before. She was just a very young and very pretty girl, telling in a low and remorseful voice of the tragic dilemma to which she had brought herself. Of Celymene all that remained was something exquisite and fragile in her beauty, in the slimness of her figure, in her daintiness of hand and foot—something almost of the hot-house. But the story she told was, detail for detail, the same which Calladine had already related.

"Thank you," said Hanaud when she had done. "Now I must ask you two questions."

"I will answer them."

Mr. Ricardo sat up. He began to think of a third question which he might put himself, something uncommonly subtle and searching, which Hanaud would never have thought of. But Hanaud put his questions, and Ricardo almost jumped out of his chair.

"You will forgive me. Miss Carew. But have you ever stolen before?"

Joan Carew turned upon Hanaud with spirit. Then a change swept over her face.

"You have a right to ask," she answered. "Never." She looked into his eyes as she answered. Hanaud did not move. He sat with a hand upon each knee and led to his second question.

"Early this morning, when you left this room, you told Mr. Calladine that you would wait at the Semiramis until he telephoned to you?"

"Yes."

"Yet when he telephoned, you had gone out?"

"Yes."

"Why?"

"I will tell you," said Joan Carew. "I could not bear to keep the little diamond chain in my room."

For a moment even Hanaud was surprised. He had lost sight of that complication. Now he leaned forward anxiously; indeed, with a greater anxiety than he had yet shown in all this affair.

"I was terrified," continued Joan Carew. "I kept thinking: 'They must have found out by now. They will search everywhere.' I didn't reason. I lay in bed expecting to hear every moment a loud knocking on the door. Besides—the chain itself being there in my bedroom—her chain—the dead woman's chain—no, I couldn't endure it. I felt as if I had stolen it. Then my maid brought in my tea."

"You had locked it away?" cried Hanaud.

"Yes. My maid did not see it."

Joan Carew explained how she had risen, dressed, wrapped the chain in a pad of cotton-wool and enclosed it in an envelope. The envelope had not the stamp of the hotel upon it. It was a rather large envelope, one of a packet which she had bought in a crowded shop in Oxford Street on her way from Euston to the Semiramis. She had bought the envelopes of that particular size in order that when she sent her letter of introduction to the Director of the Opera at Covent Garden she might enclose with it a photograph.

"And to whom did you send it?" asked Mr. Ricardo.

"To Mrs. Blumenstein at the Semiramis. I printed the address carefully. Then I went out and posted it."

"Where?" Hanaud inquired.

"In the big letter-box of the Post Office at the corner of Trafalgar Square."

Hanaud looked at the girl sharply.

"You had your wits about you, I see," he said.

"What if the envelope gets lost?" said Ricardo.

Hanuad laughed grimly.

"If one envelope is delivered at its address in London to-day, it will be that one," he said. "The news of the crime is published, you see," and he swung round to Joan.

"Did you know that, Miss Carew?"

"No," she answered in an awe-stricken voice.

"Well, then, it is. Let us see what the special investigator has to say about it." And Hanaud, with a deliberation which Mr. Ricardo found quite excruciating, spread out the newspaper on the table in front of him.

IV

There was only one new fact in the couple of columns devoted to the mystery. Mrs. Blumenstein had died from chloroform poisoning. She was of a stout habit, and the thieves were not skilled in the administration of the anaesthetic.

"It's murder none the less," said Hanaud, and he gazed straight at Joan, asking her by the direct summons of his eyes what she was going to do.

"I must tell my story to the police," she replied painfully and slowly. But she did not hesitate; she was announcing a meditated plan.

Hanaud neither agreed nor differed. His face was blank, and when he spoke there was no cordiality in his voice. "Well," he asked, "and what is it that you have to say to the police, miss? That you went into the room to steal, and that you were attacked by two strangers, dressed as apaches, and masked? That is all?"

"Yes."

"And how many men at the Semiramis ball were dressed as apaches and wore masks? Come! Make a guess. A hundred at the least?"

"I should think so."

"Then what will your confession do beyond—I quote your English idiom—putting you in the coach?"

Mr. Ricardo now smiled with relief. Hanaud was taking a definite line. His knowledge of idiomatic English might be incomplete, but his heart was in the right place. The girl traced a vague pattern on the tablecloth with her fingers.

"Yet I think I must tell the police," she repeated, looking up and dropping her eyes again. Mr. Ricardo noticed that her eyelashes were very long. For the first time Hanaud's face relaxed.

"And I think you are quite right," he cried heartily, to Mr. Ricardo's surprise. "Tell them the truth before they suspect it, and they will help you out of the affair if they can. Not a doubt of it. Come, I will go with you myself to Scotland Yard."

"Thank you," said Joan, and the pair drove away in a cab together.

Hanaud returned to Grosvenor Square alone and lunched with Ricardo.

"It was all right," he said. "The police were very kind. Miss Joan Carew told her story to them as she had told it to us. Fortunately, the envelope with the aluminium chain had already been delivered, and was in their hands. They were much mystified about it, but Miss Joan's story gave them a reasonable explanation. I think they are inclined to believe her; and, if she is speaking the truth, they will keep her out of the witness-box if they can."

"She is to stay here in London, then?" asked Ricardo.

"Oh, yes; she is not to go. She will present her letters at the Opera House and secure an engagement, if she can. The criminals might be lulled thereby into a belief that the girl had kept the whole strange incident to herself, and that there was nowhere even a knowledge of the disguise which they had used." Hanaud spoke as carelessly as if the matter was not very important; and Ricardo, with an unusual flash of shrewdness, said:

"It is clear, my friend, that you do not think those two men will ever be caught at all."

Hanaud shrugged his shoulders.

"There is always a chance. But listen. There is a room with a hundred guns, one of which is loaded. Outside the room there are a hundred pigeons, one of which is white. You are taken into the room blind-fold. You choose the loaded gun and you shoot the one white pigeon. That is the value of the chance."

"But," exclaimed Ricardo, "those pearls were of great value, and I have heard at a trial expert evidence given by pearl merchants. All agree that the pearls of great value are known; so, when they come upon the market——"

"That is true," Hanaud interrupted imperturbably. "But how are they known?"

"By their weight," said Mr. Ricardo.

"Exactly," replied Hanaud. "But did you not also hear at this trial of yours that pearls can be peeled like an onion? No? It is true. Remove a skin, two skins, the weight is altered, the pearl is a trifle smaller. It has lost a little of its value, yes—but you can no longer identify it as the so-and-so pearl which belonged to this or that sultan, was stolen by the vizier, bought by Messrs. Lustre and Steinopolis, of Hatton Garden, and subsequently sold to the wealthy Mrs. Blumenstein. No, your pearl has vanished altogether. There is a new pearl which can be traded." He looked at Ricardo. "Who shall say that those pearls are not already in one of the queer little back streets of Amsterdam, undergoing their transformation?"

Mr. Ricardo was not persuaded because he would not be. "I have some experience in these matters," he said loftily to Hanaud. "I am sure that we shall lay our hands upon the criminals. We have never failed."

Hanaud grinned from ear to ear. The only experience which Mr. Ricardo had ever had was gained on the shores of Geneva and at Aix under Hanaud's tuition. But Hanaud did not argue, and there the matter rested.

The days flew by. It was London's play-time. The green and gold of early summer deepened and darkened; wondrous warm nights under England's pale blue sky, when the streets rang with the joyous feet of youth, led in clear dawns and lovely glowing days. Hanaud made acquaintance with the wooded reaches of the Thames; Joan Carew sang "Louise" at Covent Garden with notable success; and the affair of the Semiramis Hotel, in the minds of the few who remembered it, was already added to the long list of unfathomed mysteries.

But towards the end of May there occurred a startling development. Joan Carew wrote to Mr. Ricardo that she would call upon him in the afternoon, and she begged him to secure the presence of Hanaud. She came as the clock struck; she was pale and agitated; and in the room where Calladine had first told the story of her visit she told another story which, to Mr. Ricardo's thinking, was yet more strange and—yes—yet more suspicious.

"It has been going on for some time," she began. "I thought of coming to you at once. Then I wondered whether, if I waited— oh, you'll never believe me!"

"Let us hear!" said Hanaud patiently.

"I began to dream of that room, the two men disguised and masked, the still figure in the bed. Night after night! I was terrified to go to sleep. I felt the hand upon my mouth. I used to catch myself falling asleep, and walk about the room with all the lights up to keep myself awake."

"But you couldn't," said Hanaud with a smile. "Only the old can do that."

"No, I couldn't," she admitted; "and—oh, my nights were horrible until"—she paused and looked at her companions doubtfully—"until one night the mask slipped."

"What—?" cried Hanaud, and a note of sternness rang suddenly in his voice. "What are you saying?"

With a desperate rush of words, and the colour staining her forehead and cheeks, Joan Carew continued:

"It is true. The mask slipped on the face of one of the men—of the man who held me. Only a little way; it just left his forehead visible—no more."

"Well?" asked Hanaud, and Mr. Ricardo leaned forward, swaying between the austerity of criticism and the desire to believe so thrilling a revelation.

"I waked up," the girl continued, "in the darkness, and for a moment the whole scene remained vividly with me—for just long enough for me to fix clearly in my mind the figure of the apache with the white forehead showing above the mask."

"When was that?" asked Ricardo.

"A fortnight ago."

"Why didn't you come with your story then?"

"I waited," said Joan. "What I had to tell wasn't yet helpful. I thought that another night the mask might slip lower still. Besides, I—it is difficult to describe just what I felt. I felt it important just to keep that photograph in my mind, not to think about it, not to talk about it, not even to look at it too often lest I should begin to imagine the rest of the face and find something familiar in the man's carriage and shape when there was nothing really familiar to me at all. Do you understand that?" she asked, with her eyes fixed in appeal on Hanaud's face.

"Yes," replied Hanaud. "I follow your thought."

"I thought there was a chance now—the strangest chance— that the truth might be reached. I did not wish to spoil it," and she turned eagerly to Ricardo, as if, having persuaded Hanaud, she would now turn her batteries on his companion. "My whole point of view was changed. I was no longer afraid of falling asleep lest I should dream. I wished to dream, but——"

"But you could not," suggested Hanaud.

"No, that is the truth," replied Joan Carew. "Whereas before I was anxious to keep awake and yet must sleep from sheer fatigue, now that I tried consciously to put myself to sleep I remained awake all through the night, and only towards morning, when the light was coming through the blinds, dropped off into a heavy, dreamless slumber."

Hanaud nodded.

"It is a very perverse world, Miss Carew, and things go by contraries."

Ricardo listened for some note of irony in Hanaud's voice, some look of disbelief in his face. But there was neither the one nor the other. Hanaud was listening patiently.

"Then came my rehearsals," Joan Carew continued, "and that wonderful opera drove everything else out of my head. I had such a chance, if only I could make use of it! When I went to bed now, I went with that haunting music in my ears—the call of Paris—oh, you must remember it. But can you realise what it must mean to a girl who is going to sing it for the first time in Covent Garden?"

Mr. Ricardo saw his opportunity. He, the connoisseur, to whom the psychology of the green room was as an open book, could answer that question.

"It is true, my friend," he informed Hanaud with quiet authority. "The great march of events leaves the artist cold. He lives aloof. While the tumbrils thunder in the streets he adds a delicate tint to the picture he is engaged upon or recalls his triumph in his last great part."

"Thank you," said Hanaud gravely. "And now Miss Carew may perhaps resume her story."

"It was the very night of my debut," she continued. "I had supper with some friends. A great artist. Carmen Valeri, honoured me with her presence. I went home excited, and that night I dreamed again."

"Yes?"

"This time the chin, the lips, the eyes were visible. There was only a black strip across the middle of the face. And I thought— nay, I was sure—that if that strip vanished I should know the man."

"And it did vanish?"

"Three nights afterwards."

"And you did know the man?"

The girl's face became troubled. She frowned.

"I knew the face, that was all," she answered. "I was disappointed. I had never spoken to the man. I am sure of that still. But somewhere I have seen him."

"You don't even remember when?" asked Hanaud.

"No." Joan Carew reflected for a moment with her eyes upon the carpet, and then flung up her head with a gesture of despair. "No. I try all the time to remember. But it is no good."

Mr. Ricardo could not restrain a movement of indignation. He was being played with. The girl with her fantastic story had worked him up to a real pitch of excitement only to make a fool of him. All his earlier suspicions flowed back into his mind. What if, after all, she was implicated in the murder and the theft? What if, with a perverse cunning, she had told Hanaud and himself just enough of what she knew, just enough of the truth, to persuade them to protect her? What if her frank confession of her own overpowering impulse to steal the necklace was nothing more than a subtle appeal to the sentimental pity of men, an appeal based upon a wider knowledge of men's weaknesses than a girl of nineteen or twenty ought to have? Mr. Ricardo cleared his throat and sat forward in his chair. He was girding himself for a singularly searching interrogatory when Hanaud asked the most irrelevant of questions:

"How did you pass the evening of that night when you first dreamed complete the face of your assailant?"

Joan Carew reflected. Then her face cleared.

"I know," she exclaimed. "I was at the opera."

"And what was being given?"

"*The Jewels of the Madonna.*"

Hanaud nodded his head. To Ricardo it seemed that he had expected precisely that answer.

"Now," he continued, "you are sure that you have seen this man?"

"Yes."

"Very well," said Hanaud. "There is a game you play at children's parties—is there not?—animal, vegetable, or mineral, and always you get the answer. Let us play that game for a few minutes, you and I."

Joan Carew drew up her chair to the table and sat with her chin propped upon her hands and her eyes fixed on Hanaud's face. As he put each question she pondered on it and answered. If she answered doubtfully he pressed it.

"You crossed on the *Lucania* from New York?"

"Yes."

"Picture to yourself the dining-room, the tables. You have the picture quite clear?"

"Yes."

"Was it at breakfast that you saw him?"

"No."

"At luncheon?"

"No."

"At dinner?"

She paused for a moment, summoning before her eyes the travellers at the tables.

"No."

"Not in the dining-table at all, then?"

"No."

"In the library, when you were writing letters, did you not one day lift your head and see him?"

"No."

"On the promenade deck? Did he pass you when you sat in your deck-chair, or did you pass him when he sat in his chair?"

"No."

Step by step Hanaud took her back to New York to her hotel, to journeys in the train. Then he carried her to Milan where she had studied. It was extraordinary to Ricardo to realise how much Hanaud knew of the curriculum of a student aspiring to grand opera. From Milan he brought her again to New York, and at the last, with a start of joy, she cried: "Yes, it was there."

Hanaud took his handkerchief from his pocket and wiped his forehead.

"Ouf!" he grunted. "To concentrate the mind on a day like this, it makes one hot, I can tell you. Now, Miss Carew, let us hear."

It was at a concert at the house of a Mrs. Starlingshield in Fifth Avenue and in the afternoon. Joan Carew sang. She was a stranger to New York and very nervous. She saw nothing but a mist of faces whilst she sang, but when she had finished the mist cleared, and as she left the improvised stage she saw the man. He was standing against the wall in a line of men. There was no particular reason why her eyes should single him out, except that he was paying no attention to her singing, and, indeed, she forgot him altogether afterwards.

"I just happened to see him clearly and distinctly," she said. "He was tall, clean-shaven, rather dark, not particularly young—thirty-five or so, I should say—a man with a heavy face and beginning to grow stout. He moved away whilst I was bowing to the audience, and I noticed him afterwards walking about, talking to people."

"Do you remember to whom?"

"No."

"Did he notice you, do you think?"

"I am sure he didn't," the girl replied emphatically. "He never looked at the stage where I was singing, and he never looked towards me afterwards."

She gave, so far as she could remember, the names of such guests and singers as she knew at that party. "And that is all," she said.

"Thank you," said Hanaud. "It is perhaps a good deal. But it is perhaps nothing at all."

"You will let me hear from you?" she cried, as she rose to her feet.

"Miss Carew, I am at your service," he returned. She gave him her hand timidly and he took it cordially. For Mr. Ricardo she had merely a bow, a bow which recognised that he distrusted her and that she had no right to be offended. Then she went, and Hanaud smiled across the table at Ricardo.

"Yes," he said, "all that you are thinking is true enough. A man who slips out of society to indulge a passion for a drug in greater peace, a girl who, on her own confession, tried to steal, and, to crown all, this fantastic story. It is natural to disbelieve every word of it. But we disbelieved before, when we left Calladine's lodging in the Adelphi, and we were wrong. Let us be warned."

"You have an idea?" exclaimed Ricardo.

"Perhaps!" said Hanaud. And he looked down the theatre column of the *Times*. "Let us distract ourselves by going to the theatre."

"You are the most irritating man!" Mr. Ricardo broke out impulsively. "If I had to paint your portrait, I should paint you with your finger against the side of your nose, saying mysteriously: '*I* know,' when you know nothing at all."

Hanaud made a schoolboy's grimace. "We will go and sit in your box at the opera to-night," he said, "and you shall explain to me all through the beautiful music the theory of the tonic sol-fa."

They reached Covent Garden before the curtain rose. Mr. Ricardo's box was on the lowest tier and next to the omnibus box.

"We are near the stage," said Hanaud, as he took his seat in the corner and so arranged the curtain that he could see and yet was hidden from view. "I like that."

The theatre was full; stalls and boxes shimmered with jewels and satin, and all that was famous that season for beauty and distinction had made its tryst there that night.

"Yes, this is wonderful," said Hanaud. "What opera do they play?" He glanced at his programme and cried, with a little start of surprise: "We are in luck. It is *The Jewels of the Madonna.*"

"Do you believe in omens?" Mr. Ricardo asked coldly. He had not yet recovered from his rebuff of the afternoon.

"No, but I believe that Carmen Valeri is at her best in this part," said Hanaud.

Mr. Ricardo belonged to that body of critics which must needs spoil your enjoyment by comparisons and recollections of other great artists. He was at a disadvantage certainly to-night, for the opera was new. But he did his best. He imagined others in the part, and when the great scene came at the end of the second act, and Carmen Valeri, on obtaining from her lover the jewels stolen from the sacred image, gave such a display of passion as fairly enthralled that audience, Mr. Ricardo sighed quietly and patiently.

"How Calve would have brought out the psychological value of that scene!" he murmured; and he was quite vexed with Hanaud, who sat with his opera glasses held to his eyes, and every sense apparently concentrated on the stage. The curtains rose and rose again when the act was concluded, and still Hanaud sat motionless as the Sphynx, staring through his glasses.

"That is all," said Ricardo when the curtains fell for the fifth time.

"They will come out," said Hanaud. "Wait!" And from between the curtains Carmen Valeri was led out into the full glare of the footlights with the panoply of jewels flashing on her breast. Then at last Hanaud put down his glasses and turned to Ricardo with a look of exultation and genuine delight upon his face which filled that season-worn dilettante with envy.

"What a night!" said Hanaud. "What a wonderful night!" And he applauded until he split his gloves. At the end of the opera he cried: "We will go and take supper at the Semiramis. Yes, my friend, we will finish our evening like gallant gentlemen. Come! Let us not think of the morning." And boisterously he slapped Ricardo in the small of the back.

In spite of his boast, however, Hanaud hardly touched his supper, and he played with, rather than drank, his brandy and soda. He had a little table to which he was accustomed beside a glass screen in the depths of the room, and he sat with his back to the wall watching the groups which poured in. Suddenly his face lighted up.

"Here is Carmen Valeri!" he cried. "Once more we are in luck. Is it not that she is beautiful?"

Mr. Ricardo turned languidly about in his chair and put up his eyeglass.

"So, so," he said.

"Ah!" returned Hanaud. "Then her companion will interest you still more. For he is the man who murdered Mrs. Blumenstein."

Mr. Ricardo jumped so that his eyeglass fell down and tinkled on its cord against the buttons of his waistcoat.

"What!" he exclaimed. "It's impossible!" He looked again. "Certainly the man fits Joan Carew's description. But—" He turned back to Hanaud utterly astounded. And as he looked at the Frenchman all his earlier recollections of him, of his swift deductions, of the subtle imagination which his heavy body so well concealed, crowded in upon Ricardo and convinced him.

"How long have you known?" he asked in a whisper of awe.

"Since ten o'clock to-night."

"But you will have to find the necklace before you can prove it."

"The necklace!" said Hanaud carelessly. "That is already found."

Mr. Ricardo had been longing for a thrill. He had it now. He felt it in his very spine.

"It's found?" he said in a startled whisper.

"Yes."

Ricardo turned again, with as much indifference as he could assume, towards the couple who were settling down at their table, the man with a surly indifference, Carmen Valeri with the radiance of a woman who has just achieved a triumph and is now free to enjoy the fruits of it. Confusedly, recollections returned to Ricardo of questions put that afternoon by Hanaud to Joan Carew—subtle questions into which the name of Carmen Valeri was continually entering. She was a woman of thirty, certainly beautiful, with a clear, pale face and eyes like the night.

"Then she is implicated too!" he said. What a change for her, he thought, from the stage of Covent Garden to the felon's cell, from the gay supper-room of the Semiramis, with its bright frocks and its babel of laughter, to the silence and the ignominious garb of the workrooms in Aylesbury Prison!

"She!" exclaimed Hanaud; and in his passion for the contrasts of drama Ricardo was almost disappointed. "She has nothing whatever to do with it. She knows nothing. Andre Favart there—yes. But Carmen Valeri! She's as stupid as an owl, and loves him beyond words. Do you want to know how stupid she is? You shall know. I asked Mr. Clements, the director of the opera house, to take supper with us, and here he is."

Hanaud stood up and shook hands with the director. He was of the world of business rather than of art, and long experience of the ways of tenors and prima-donnas had given him a good-humoured cynicism.

"They are spoilt children, all tantrums and vanity," he said, "and they would ruin you to keep a rival out of the theatre."

He told them anecdote upon anecdote.

"And Carmen Valeri," Hanaud asked in a pause; "is she troublesome this season?"

"Has been," replied Clements dryly. "At present she is playing at being good. But she gave me a turn some weeks ago." He turned to Ricardo. "Superstition's her trouble, and Andre Favart knows it. She left him behind in America this spring."

"America!" suddenly cried Ricardo; so suddenly that Clements looked at him in surprise.

"She was singing in New York, of course, during the winter," he returned. "Well, she left him behind, and I was shaking hands with myself when he began to deal the cards over there. She came to me in a panic. She had just had a cable. She couldn't sing on Friday night. There was a black knave next to the nine of diamonds. She wouldn't sing for worlds. And it was the first night of *The Jewels of the Madonna!* Imagine the fix I was in!"

"What did you do?" asked Ricardo.

"The only thing there was to do," replied Clements with a shrug of the shoulders. "I cabled Favart some money and he dealt the cards again. She came to me beaming. Oh, she had been so distressed to put me in the cart! But what could she do? Now there was a red queen next to the ace of hearts, so she could sing without a scruple so long, of course, as she didn't pass a funeral on the way down to the opera house. Luckily she didn't. But my money brought Favart over here, and now I'm living on a volcano. For he's the greatest scoundrel unhung. He never has a farthing, however much she gives him; he's a blackmailer, he's a swindler, he has no manners and no graces, he looks like a butcher and treats her as if she were dirt, he never goes near the opera except when she is singing in this part, and she worships the ground he walks on. Well, I suppose it's time to go."

The lights had been turned off, the great room was emptying. Mr. Ricardo and his friends rose to go, but at the door Hanaud detained Mr. Clements, and they talked together alone for some little while, greatly to Mr. Ricardo's annoyance. Hanaud's good humour, however, when he rejoined his friend, was enough for two.

"I apologise, my friend, with my hand on my heart. But it was for your sake that I stayed behind. You have a meretricious taste for melodrama which I deeply deplore, but which I mean to gratify. I ought to leave for Paris to-morrow, but I shall not. I shall stay until Thursday." And he skipped upon the pavement as they walked home to Grosvenor Square.

Mr. Ricardo bubbled with questions, but he knew his man. He would get no answer to any one of them to-night. So he worked out the problem for himself as he lay awake in his bed, and he came down to breakfast next morning fatigued but triumphant. Hanaud was already chipping off the top of his egg at the table.

"So I see you have found it all out, my friend," he said.

"Not all," replied Ricardo modestly, "and you will not mind, I am sure, if I follow the usual custom and wish you a good morning."

"Not at all," said Hanaud. "I am all for good manners myself."

He dipped his spoon into his egg.

"But I am longing to hear the line of your reasoning."

Mr. Ricardo did not need much pressing.

"Joan Carew saw Andre Favart at Mrs. Starlingshield's party, and saw him with Carmen Valeri. For Carmen Valeri was there. I remember that you asked Joan for the names of the artists who sang, and Carmen Valeri was amongst them."

Hanaud nodded his head.

"Exactly."

"No doubt Joan Carew noticed Carmen Valeri particularly, and so took unconsciously into her mind an impression of the man who was with her, Andre Favart—of his build, of his walk, of his type."

Again Hanaud agreed.

"She forgets the man altogether, but the picture remains latent in her mind—an undeveloped film."

Hanaud looked up in surprise, and the surprise flattered Mr. Ricardo. Not for nothing had he tossed about in his bed for the greater part of the night.

"Then came the tragic night at the Semiramis. She does not consciously recognise her assailant, but she dreams the scene again and again, and by a process of unconscious cerebration the figure of the man becomes familiar. Finally she makes her debut, is entertained at supper afterwards, and meets once more Carmen Valeri."

"Yes, for the first time since Mrs. Starlingshield's party," interjected Hanaud.

"She dreams again, she remembers asleep more than she remembers when awake. The presence of Carmen Valeri at her supper-party has its effect. By a process of association, she recalls Favart, and the mask slips on the face of her assailant. Some days later she goes to the opera. She hears Carmen Valeri sing in *The Jewels of the Madonna*. No doubt the passion of her acting, which I am more prepared to acknowledge this morning than I was last night, affects Joan Carew powerfully, emotionally. She goes to bed with her head full of Carmen Valeri, and she dreams not of Carmen Valeri, but of the man who is unconsciously associated with Carmen Valeri in her thoughts. The mask vanishes altogether. She sees her assailant now, has his portrait limned in her mind, would know him if she met him in the street, though she does not know by what means she identified him."

"Yes," said Hanaud. "It is curious the brain working while the body sleeps, the dream revealing what thought cannot recall."

Mr. Ricardo was delighted. He was taken seriously.

"But of course," he said, "I could not have worked the problem out but for you. You knew of Andre Favart and the kind of man he was."

Hanaud laughed.

"Yes. That is always my one little advantage. I know all the cosmopolitan blackguards of Europe." His laughter ceased suddenly, and he brought his clenched fist heavily down upon the table. "Here is one of them who will be very well out of the world, my friend," he said very quietly, but there was a look of force in his face and a hard light in his eyes which made Mr. Ricardo shiver.

For a few moments there was silence. Then Ricardo asked: "But have you evidence enough?"

"Yes."

"Your two chief witnesses, Calladine and Joan Carew—you said it yourself—there are facts to discredit them. Will they be believed?"

"But they won't appear in the case at all," Hanaud said. "Wait, wait!" and once more he smiled. "By the way, what is the number of Calladine's house?"

Ricardo gave it, and Hanaud therefore wrote a letter. "It is all for your sake, my friend," he said with a chuckle.

"Nonsense," said Ricardo. "You have the spirit of the theatre in your bones."

"Well, I shall not deny it," said Hanaud, and he sent out the letter to the nearest pillar-box.

Mr. Ricardo waited in a fever of impatience until Thursday came. At breakfast Hanaud would talk of nothing but the news of the day. At luncheon he was no better. The affair of the Semiramis Hotel seemed a thousand miles from any of his thoughts. But at five o'clock he said as he drank his tea:

"You know, of course, that we go to the opera to-night?"

"Yes. Do we?"

"Yes. Your young friend Calladine, by the way, will join us in your box."

"That is very kind of him, I am sure," said Mr. Ricardo.

The two men arrived before the rising of the curtain, and in the crowded lobby a stranger spoke a few words to Hanaud, but what he said Ricardo could not hear. They took their seats in the box, and Hanaud looked at his programme.

"Ah! It is *Il Ballo de Maschera* to-night. We always seem to hit upon something appropriate, don't we?"

Then he raised his eyebrows.

"Oh-o! Do you see that our pretty young friend, Joan Carew, is singing in the role of the page? It is a showy part. There is a particular melody with a long-sustained trill in it, as far as I remember."

Mr. Ricardo was not deceived by Hanaud's apparent ignorance of the opera to be given that night and of the part Joan Carew was to take. He was, therefore, not surprised when Hanaud added:

"By the way, I should let Calladine find it all out for himself."

Mr. Ricardo nodded sagely.

"Yes. That is wise. I had thought of it myself." But he had done nothing of the kind. He was only aware that the elaborate stage-management in which Hanaud delighted was working out to the desired climax, whatever that climax might be. Calladine entered the box a few minutes later and shook hands with them awkwardly.

"It was kind of you to invite me," he said and, very ill at ease, he took a seat between them and concentrated his attention on the house as it filled up.

"There's the overture," said Hanaud. The curtains divided and were festooned on either side of the stage. The singers came on in their turn; the page appeared to a burst of delicate applause (Joan Carew had made a small name for herself that season), and with a stifled cry Calladine shot back in the box as if he had been struck. Even then Mr. Ricardo did not understand. He only realised that Joan Carew was looking extraordinarily trim and smart in her boy's dress. He had to look from his programme to the stage and back again several times before the reason of Calladine's exclamation dawned on him. When it did, he was horrified. Hanaud, in his craving for dramatic effects, must have lost his head altogether. Joan Carew was wearing, from the ribbon in her hair to the scarlet heels of her buckled satin shoes, the same dress as she had worn on the tragic night at the Semiramis Hotel. He leaned forward in his agitation to Hanaud.

"You must be mad. Suppose Favart is in the theatre and sees her. He'll be over on the Continent by one in the morning."

"No, he won't," replied Hanaud. "For one thing, he never comes to Covent Garden unless one opera, with Carmen Valeri in the chief part, is being played, as you heard the other night at supper. For a second thing, he isn't in the house. I know where he is. He is gambling in Dean Street, Soho. For a third thing, my friend, he couldn't leave by the nine o'clock train for the Continent if he wanted to. Arrangements have been made. For a fourth thing, he wouldn't wish to. He has really remarkable reasons for desiring to stay in London. But he will come to the theatre later. Clements will send him an urgent message, with the result that he will go straight to Clements' office. Meanwhile, we can enjoy ourselves, eh?"

Never was the difference between the amateur dilettante and the genuine professional more clearly exhibited than by the behaviour of the two men during the rest of the performance. Mr. Ricardo might have been sitting on a coal fire from his jumps and twistings; Hanaud stolidly enjoyed the music, and when Joan Carew sang her famous solo his hands clamoured for an encore louder than anyone's in the boxes. Certainly, whether excitement was keeping her up or no, Joan Carew had never sung better in her life. Her voice was clear and fresh as a bird's—a bird with a soul inspiring its song. Even Calladine drew his chair forward again and sat with his eyes fixed upon the stage and quite carried out of himself. He drew a deep breath at the end.

"She is wonderful," he said, like a man waking up.

"She is very good," replied Mr. Ricardo, correcting Calladine's transports.

"We will go round to the back of the stage," said Hanaud.

They passed through the iron door and across the stage to a long corridor with a row of doors on one side. There were two or three men standing about in evening dress, as if waiting for friends in the dressing-rooms. At the third door Hanaud stopped and knocked. The door was opened by Joan Carew, still dressed in her green and gold. Her face was troubled, her eyes afraid.

"Courage, little one," said Hanaud, and he slipped past her into the room. "It is as well that my ugly, familiar face should not be seen too soon."

The door closed and one of the strangers loitered along the corridor and spoke to a call-boy. The call-boy ran off. For five minutes more Mr. Ricardo waited with a beating heart. He had the joy of a man in the centre of things. All those people driving homewards in their motor-cars along the Strand—how he pitied them! Then, at the end of the corridor, he saw Clements and Andre Favart. They approached, discussing the possibility of Carmen Valeri's appearance in London opera during the next season.

"We have to look ahead, my dear friend," said Clements, "and though I should be extremely sorry——"

At that moment they were exactly opposite Joan Carew's door. It opened, she came out; with a nervous movement she shut the door behind her. At the sound Andre Favart turned, and he saw drawn up against the panels of the door, with a look of terror in her face, the same gay figure which had interrupted him in Mrs. Blumenstein's bedroom. There was no need for Joan to act. In the presence of this man her fear was as real as it had been on the night of the Semiramis ball. She trembled from head to foot. Her eyes closed; she seemed about to swoon.

Favart stared and uttered an oath. His face turned white; he staggered back as if he had seen a ghost. Then he made a wild dash along the corridor, and was seized and held by two of the men in evening dress. Favart recovered his wits. He ceased to struggle.

"What does this outrage mean?" he asked, and one of the men drew a warrant and notebook from his pocket.

"You are arrested for the murder of Mrs. Blumenstein in the Semiramis Hotel," he said, "and I have to warn you that anything you may say will be taken down and may be used in evidence against you."

"Preposterous!" exclaimed Favart. "There's a mistake. We will go along to the police and put it right. Where's your evidence against me?"

Hanaud stepped out of the doorway of the dressing-room.

"In the property-room of the theatre," he said.

At the sight of him Favart uttered a violent cry of rage. "You are here, too, are you?" he screamed, and he sprang at Hanaud's throat. Hanaud stepped lightly aside. Favart was borne down to the ground, and when he stood up again the handcuffs were on his wrists.

Favart was led away, and Hanaud turned to Mr. Ricardo and Clements.

"Let us go to the property-room," he said. They passed along the corridor, and Ricardo noticed that Calladine was no longer with them. He turned and saw him standing outside Joan Carew's dressing-room.

"He would like to come, of course," said Ricardo.

"Would he?" asked Hanaud. "Then why doesn't he? He's quite grown up, you know," and he slipped his arm through Ricardo's and led him back across the stage. In the property-room there was already a detective in plain clothes. Mr. Ricardo had still not as yet guessed the truth.

"What is it you really want, sir?" the property-master asked of the director.

"Only the jewels of the Madonna," Hanaud answered.

The property-master unlocked a cupboard and took from it the sparkling cuirass. Hanaud pointed to it, and there, lost amongst the huge glittering stones of paste and false pearls, Mrs. Blumenstein's necklace was entwined.

"Then that is why Favart came always to Covent Garden when *The Jewels of the Madonna* was being performed!" exclaimed Ricardo.

Hanaud nodded.

"He came to watch over his treasure."

Ricardo was piecing together the sections of the puzzle.

"No doubt he knew of the necklace in America. No doubt he followed it to England."

Hanaud agreed.

"Mrs. Blumenstein's jewels were quite famous in New York."

"But to hide them here!" cried Mr. Clements. "He must have been mad."

"Why?" asked Hanaud. "Can you imagine a safer hiding-place? Who is going to burgle the property-room of Covent Garden? Who is going to look for a priceless string of pearls amongst the stage jewels of an opera house?"

"You did," said Mr. Ricardo.

"I?" replied Hanaud, shrugging his shoulders. "Joan Carew's dreams led me to Andre Favart. The first time we came here and saw the pearls of the Madonna, I was on the look-out, naturally. I noticed Favart at the back of the stalls. But it was a stroke of luck that I noticed those pearls through my opera glasses."

"At the end of the second act?" cried Ricardo suddenly. "I remember now."

"Yes," replied Hanaud. "But for that second act the pearls would have stayed comfortably here all through the season. Carmen Valeri—a fool as I told you—would have tossed them about in her dressing-room without a notion of their value, and at the end of July, when the murder at the Semiramis Hotel had been forgotten, Favart would have taken them to Amsterdam and made his bargain."

"Shall we go?"

They left the theatre together and walked down to the grill-room of the Semiramis. But as Hanaud looked through the glass door he drew back.

"We will not go in, I think, eh?"

"Why?" asked Ricardo.

Hanaud pointed to a table. Calladine and Joan Carew were seated at it taking their supper.

"Perhaps," said Hanaud with a smile, "perhaps, my friend— what? Who shall say that the rooms in the Adelphi will not be given up?"

They turned away from the hotel. But Hanaud was right, and before the season was over Mr. Ricardo had to put his hand in his pocket for a wedding present.

RESURRECTED PRESS CLASSIC MYSTERY CATALOGUE

E. C. Bentley
Trent's Last Case: The Woman in Black

Ernest Bramah
Max Carrados Resurrected:
The Detective Stories of Max Carrados

Agatha Christie
The Secret Adversary
The Mysterious Affair at Styles

Octavus Roy Cohen
Midnight

Freeman Wills Croft
The Ponson Case
The Pit Prop Syndicate

J. S. Fletcher
The Herapath Property
The Rayner-Slade Amalgamation
The Chestermarke Instinct
The Paradise Mystery
Dead Men's Money
The Middle of Things
Ravensdene Court
Scarhaven Keep
The Orange-Yellow Diamond
The Middle Temple Murder
The Tallyrand Maxim
The Borough Treasurer
In the Mayor's Parlour
The Saftey Pin

R. Austin Freeman

The Mystery of 31 New Inn from the Dr. Thorndyke Series
John Thorndyke's Cases from the Dr. Thorndyke Series
The Red Thumb Mark from The Dr. Thorndyke Series
The Eye of Osiris from The Dr. Thorndyke Series
A Silent Witness from the Dr. John Thorndyke Series
The Cat's Eye from the Dr. John Thorndyke Series
Helen Vardon's Confession: A Dr. John Thorndyke Story
As a Thief in the Night: A Dr. John Thorndyke Story
Mr. Pottermack's Oversight: A Dr. John Thorndyke Story
Dr. Thorndyke Intervenes: A Dr. John Thorndyke Story
The Singing Bone: The Adventures of Dr. Thorndyke
The Stoneware Monkey: A Dr. John Thorndyke Story
*The Great Portrait Mystery, and Other Stories: A Collection of
Dr. John Thorndyke and Other Stories*
The Penrose Mystery: A Dr. John Thorndyke Story
The Uttermost Farthing: A Savant's Vendetta

Arthur Griffiths

The Passenger From Calais
The Rome Express

Fergus Hume

The Mystery of a Hansom Cab
The Green Mummy
The Silent House
The Secret Passage

Edgar Jepson

The Loudwater Mystery

A. E. W. Mason

At the Villa Rose

A. A. Milne

The Red House Mystery

Baroness Emma Orczy

The Old Man in the Corner

Edgar Allan Poe
The Detective Stories of Edgar Allan Poe

Arthur J. Rees
The Hampstead Mystery
The Shrieking Pit
The Hand In The Dark
The Moon Rock
The Mystery of the Downs

Mary Roberts Rinehart
Sight Unseen and The Confession

Dorothy L. Sayers
Whose Body?

Sir William Magnay
The Hunt Ball Mystery

Mabel and Paul Thorne
The Sheridan Road Mystery

Louis Tracy
The Strange Case of Mortimer Fenley
The Albert Gate Mystery
The Bartlett Mystery
The Postmaster's Daughter
The House of Peril
The Sandling Case: What Would You Have Done?
Charles Edmonds Walk
The Paternoster Ruby

John R. Watson
The Mystery of the Downs
The Hampstead Mystery

Edgar Wallace
The Daffodil Mystery
The Crimson Circle

And much more!
Visit ResurrectedPress.com for our complete
catalogue

About Resurrected Press

A division of Intrepid Ink, LLC, Resurrected Press is dedicated to bringing high quality, vintage books back into publication. See our entire catalogue and find out more at www.ResurrectedPress.com.

About Intrepid Ink, LLC

Intrepid Ink, LLC provides full publishing services to authors of fiction and non-fiction books, eBooks and websites. From editing to formatting, from publishing to marketing, Intrepid Ink gets your creative works into the hands of the people who want to read them. Find out more at www.IntrepidInk.com.

www.ingramcontent.com/pod-product-compliance
Lightning Source LLC
Chambersburg PA
CBHW060933180626
46817CB00004B/1517